I0607541

Stranglehold

A Tale of Seduction, Prejudice & Murder

C. M. Grimes

S & H Publishing, Inc.
Purcellville, Virginia USA

S & H Publishing, Inc.
P. O. Box 456
Purcellville, VA 20134
www.sandhpublishing.com

Publisher's Note: This is a work of fiction. Names, characters, places, and incidents are a product of the author's imagination. Locales and public names are sometimes used for atmospheric purposes. Any resemblance to actual people, living or dead, or to businesses, companies, events, institutions, or locales is completely coincidental.

Ordering Information:
Quantity discounts are available. For details, contact the "Special Sales Department" at the address above or email sales@sandhpublishing.com.

Stranglehold / C M Grimes
ISBN 978-1-63320-056-2 Print Edition
ISBN 978-1-63320-055-5 Ebook Edition

DEDICATION

To my late uncle, David P. Grimes, an honorable man, who chased the bad guys during the glory days of crime-fighting.

Prologue

DEMONS ALWAYS VISITED HER AT NIGHT, when dark thoughts kept her from sleep. Last night proved to be no different from the rest. Past transgressions, her husband's infidelity, and the unfortunate murder continued to plague her, overwhelming her to the point of exhaustion. But still sleep would not come. The night had become her enemy, and pacing the dim hallways of her empty house provided no comfort.

But morning broke, and the woman sat at her mirror in her silk dressing gown, combing her hair, while planning a shopping trip to the city later that Saturday morning. She had an uneasy feeling that her past was catching up with her, giving much reason for worry. Her husband knew little about her father or her mother, save for the fact Mother died in a boating accident six months after Father's untimely death.

She walked to the bed where her husband slept. He'd come in late last night, and she'd pretended to be asleep. Now questions popped into her head, screaming for answers. There must be another woman. Had there been others? She put her hands over her ears, drowning out the voices. He really shouldn't have come home so late. She watched him sleeping, gently stroked his cheek, and for a brief moment imagined him dead.

She glanced at yesterday's New York Times on her husband's nightstand. Front page news declared the

Stranglehold

Allied forces were hanging Nazi leaders in Nuremberg for war crimes. She reasoned they were guilty of crimes against humanity and deserved to die, but much to her relief, she saw no blood on her hands.

Chapter 1

FRANK KOWALSKI DREAMED ABOUT BEING A COP ever since he was a kid, and he'd never once looked back. Every day like clockwork, he parked his cruiser, walked to the Twentieth Precinct and climbed the steps to a red brick building, the place he'd called home for over twenty years. Today the place was already crawling with cops, prostitutes and thugs.   He sat at his desk and put out his third cigarette of the day; it was only eight thirty A.M. At fifty- two, he was overweight, losing what little hair he had left, and not getting any younger. Suspect sketches, old newspapers, remnants from yesterday's lunch, and fingerprint evidence from a big jewelry heist in upper Manhattan littered his desk. He'd interviewed the store owner twice, as well as a very nervous clerk; with no forced entry, he was convinced it was an inside job.

The way Frank saw it: only two people had access to the wall safe—one owner and one clerk. He'd found only one set of fingerprints inside the safe that held the priceless jewelry after store hours. The loot had been taken from a large metal jewelry box—also with one set of prints. The safe also contained a substantial theft insurance policy.

So Frank figured that the "rat," better known as the sole store clerk, had fingered his boss, a rich man who got behind in his alimony payments and thought it was okay to defraud the insurance company. When he knew the cops were hot on his trail, he'd made a tearful confession to his ex-wife, crying like a baby. So the disgruntled wife put the final nail in his coffin and he didn't even see it coming. Stupid bastard—guaranteed at least twenty years in the slammer. He coulda told him. And to top it all off, putting the blame on some poor young clerk. But like Frank always said, the prints tell the story and they never lie.

Frank sat back in his chair, put his feet up on the desk and looked around the station. Two hookers from the Bronx were being booked for the second time in less than a week, hollering all the way to a holding cell. A two-bit bookie, screaming that he was legit, begged for his lawyer, and an unshaven madman was being charged with beating the daylights out of his old lady. Between the noise, the clacking typewriters and the endless circus of criminals, he might have lost his mind a long time ago. But although the crap never seemed to end, Frank had to admit he loved every minute of it.

Since he'd had been promoted to Detective Specialist a little over a month ago, the only real case worth working on was the jewelry caper that was about to come to a close. Maybe being a beat cop hadn't been so bad after all. He'd been out on the street—protecting the fine men and women of his city. And just maybe being a detective wasn't what it was cracked up to be.

Captain Smallwood walked in, startling Frank. He reluctantly took his feet off the desk and grinned at his boss.

"You got the arrest warrant, Boss?" Frank asked.

"Signed, sealed and ready to be delivered," the captain replied.

"You gotta know he's gonna pee himself when I cuff him. He thinks I'm coming to get his 'faithful' employee."

"Yeah, I've been thinking. What's going to happen to that poor kid after the store closes down?"

"Joe could always use another dishwasher at Duffy's. I think he's too young to serve booze."

"I know I've said this before Frankie, but you're one helluva guy."

"You don't think I already knew that?"

Chapter 2

BOBBY JOHN TAYLOR HAD BIG DREAMS. Maybe that was why he was so upset about the way he felt about his place in the world. Three years ago, his Uncle Louis recruited him to be a police officer in Harlem's Thirty-Fourth Precinct, where his uncle had proudly served for over twelve years. And Bobby John was thankful. The job kept him out of trouble and out of jail. He actually liked being a beat cop and spending time with his uncle, the only male role model B.J. ever remembered. Uncle Louis even introduced him to his ex-wife.

Bobby John always felt he had a real shot in the world, but his temper always seemed to get the best of him. His short fuse was the reason he never finished high school.

It happened when Danny Esposito called his mama a whore out behind the school when they were having a smoke. Bobby John damn near beat him to death and was told to leave the school and never come back. Nobody, but nobody, disrespected his mama like that. He never stopped missing her. She was a woman who cleaned rich white folk's houses until she could barely climb the two stories to her apartment. She read the scriptures every night, trusted Jesus and tried to bring her son up right. And he had deeply disappointed her. That's when Uncle Louis stepped in and changed his life for the better.

His uncle Louis was also involved in the Guardians Association, a group that worked on getting equal treatment for Negro police officers. Since some of the big shots in the Thirty-Fourth didn't go along with all their ideas, some of them met secretly in Harlem's Y.M.C.A. once a month. Bobby John knew he had to keep that to himself, but he felt frustrated and angry. He understood the principles of the Guardians, but he didn't agree with most of them. He also knew that he could learn a lot working with a white officer, but that was practically unheard of. Uncle Louis called it "crazy talk." Maybe it was. One thing B.J. did agree on was that equal treatment for the colored man would be a long time coming. And for that simple reason, he kept coming back.

Bobby John arrived late at the Wednesday night meeting. He sat in the back of the room so as not to be noticed. Already two of the veteran officers of the Thirty-Fourth were having a heated argument. He tried to listen for the better part of an hour, when he'd heard enough. He planned to slip out of the room when he got the chance and head for the front door without being seen.

***

Frank pulled up in front of the impressive brick building and turned off his headlights. A big waste of time, a wild goose chase, he thought. But the captain was a rational man. If he wanted something checked out, Frank was the one to do it. Especially, since he'd put the jewelry store robbery to rest. Something was definitely going on at Harlem's Y.M.C.A., but what? Captain Smallwood thought it might be a police matter worth checking out and Frank had no criminals to chase.

People began exiting the building. Classes were ending. He headed up the steps through throngs of people, and walked through the front door, then down a long dim corridor. A colored janitor shot him a disapproving look. Frank continued to walk towards the muffled voices coming from the room directly in front of him. Nothing seemed suspicious or worth breaking up.

He decided to go outside for a cigarette, and wait for things to finish up inside. Waiting was against his nature, but he wanted to come back to the station in the morning with some answers for his boss.

Less than a half hour later, around ten o'clock, the front door opened and a young Negro police officer came down the steps and headed for the street. Not wanting to startle him, Frank coughed as he stomped out his cigarette on the concrete.

The colored officer spoke first. "A little late for a walk, especially in this neighborhood."

"Yeah, my captain asked me to check out possible illegal activity here at the 'Y.'" Frank offered his hand.

"Frank Kowalski, detective with the Two-Zero. Nice to meet you."

"Bobby John Taylor with the Three-Four," he replied with a firm handshake.

"Would you happen to know what's going on in there, if you don't mind me asking? You know--the activity coming from the first floor. I guess you do know the building is closed for the night."

"Just some police officers coming together to protect their own. Nothing illegal. I guess they just don't trust men like you to give them a fair deal, so they meet in private."

"Men like me?" asked an incredulous Frank. "What about you? I see you're leaving early."

"I guess I think it makes no sense to keep people apart, when they could get more done working together," Bobby John said.

"Maybe you're right. It doesn't make any sense. I'll tell you what. It just so happens my partner just retired. Maybe you could fill in for him for awhile until I find a replacement. I gotta tell you. Harry and I have been together for almost eleven years. It's going to be real tough to fill his shoes."

"Whoa…you gotta be kidding? I don't even know you, and you sure as hell don't know me."

"You gotta start somewhere, right? And by the looks of things, you leaving the meeting and all, you're up for a change. Not to get all sappy on you or anything, but just maybe we were supposed to meet. Why don't we talk sometime? Just come up to the Two-Zero and ask for me."

"What are you going to tell your captain—about the secret meetings and all?" a somber B.J. asked.

"Just a bunch of old ladies playing Friday night bingo. Nothing to worry about."

Bobby John smiled nervously. "I'll be seeing you, man." He disappeared down the dark street and slipped into an alley.

Chapter 3

EARLY MONDAY MORNING, ONE WEEK LATER, Bobby John Taylor walked into the Twentieth Precinct. Dressed in full uniform, he made his way through a crowd of curious officers and staff, who eventually directed him to Frank. Bobby John found him sitting at his desk, surrounded by piles of clutter and what looked like a half-eaten sandwich. Frank was busy admiring a luxury watch, one of approximately three thousand watches stashed in a Brooklyn warehouse, waiting to be fenced by the Mafia in the city and its boroughs. Distributing hot watches by mob goons was one of their less sordid crimes; he was glad that he didn't have to deal with mobsters sucking the life out of his city.

Frank looked up, surprised to see Bobby John standing over him.

"Maybe this was just a bad idea, Detective Kowalski," Bobby John said. "I got pretty much dirty looks from some of your buddies ever since I walked in. It don't look like your friends are in the habit of seeing a colored man around here, unless he's bein' booked for holding up a liquor store or somethin'."

"Sorry about that Officer Taylor. Please, just call me Frank. Come on. Why don't we talk in the captain's office, where we can have some privacy?"

Frank got up and directed B.J. to the empty office directly across from his desk. They entered the room,

Frank shut the blinds and ushered Bobby John to a chair at a large desk.

"This isn't going to work. You know—you and me."

"Whadaya mean, it isn't going to work?"

"You and me and the lynch mob outside this office."

"Don't let 'em get to you. You have every reason to be here. I personally invited you, if you don't remember."

"Yeah, right--pretty damn easy for you to say. You're not the colored man who don't know his place. Did I tell you about my cousin, Larry, who got dragged behind a truck by a bunch of white men and hung outside of town just one mile from his house? You wanna know his crime, Detective? Lookin' at a white girl walkin' down the street. Not touchin' her, not talkin' to her—just lookin'."

"I'm so sorry." Frank realized his apology sounded hollow, but he'd still offered.

"Look man, this isn't the time and definitely not the place. Gotta get to work. I just hope I can leave with no trouble," Bobby John said anxiously. He got up and headed for the door.

"Bobby John, please, wait a minute. Look, you just got here. How about we meet in neutral territory? Say… tomorrow night? Ten o'clock at the 'Y.' Let's just say we have unfinished business."

"To tell you the truth, right now, I'm not even thinking about unfinished business. I'm just thinking about getting out of here without a fight."

"Okay, fair enough. Just tell me you'll meet me tomorrow night."

Bobby John hesitated for a moment. "I'll be there. I just hope it won't be a mistake."

Frank stood and parted the blinds. More than a few curious officers milled around outside Captain Smallwood's office trying to look busy. He ushered Bobby John out of the office and confronted the distrustful crowd.

"Clear the way for my friend, fellas. He's got a job to do at the Three-Four," Frank yelled. The crowd parted as Bobby John brusquely walked out of the station and headed for freedom.

A loud voice boomed out from the back of the room. Frank knew that voice.

"Who's the colored boy, Frankie? Your new partner?"

It didn't take long for raucous laughter to take over the squad room.

"Yeah, Zimmerman, as a matter-of-fact, he is. He just doesn't know it yet."

Frank went back to his desk and tried to concentrate, but he was much too irritated to get any work done, and he felt the eyes of the enemy on him. He finally got up and went to the john for a cigarette. After an unsatisfying smoke, he walked over to the sink and splashed cold water on his face. He still didn't feel any better.

He was about to leave the bathroom when Zimmerman walked into the room and took a leak in the urinal, not wasting any time starting a fight with an already angry Frank.

"Kowalski, we all know that colored boy don't belong here."

"I take it you're speaking for the whole department?"

"There's talk goin' around, and I'm telling you, it ain't pretty."

"I'm pretty damn sure who's doing all the talking."

12

"I'm just sayin', you better watch your step."

"Are you threatening me, Zimmerman?"

Johnny Zimmerman stormed out of the door, without answering.

Frank hated to admit Zimmerman might be right. It was a long shot and Bobby John probably wouldn't show up anyway. Damn Zimmerman.

Back at his desk, it seemed like everyone was watching his every move, but maybe it was paranoia talking. Frank knew he had to cool off. The entire precinct knew that Zimmerman was a bigot and could be a real asshole. There was no arguing that fact. After one too many drinks at Duffy's after work one night, Frank overheard him say that colored pimps, prostitutes, and police officers were still only niggers. Zimmerman had a way of getting everybody all riled up and listening to whatever he said. That didn't sit well with Frank.

But in spite of his big mouth, Zimmerman was basically a good cop, had been around awhile, and carried a lot of weight in the precinct. But he intimidated some of the younger officers new to the force, and he'd had more than a few run-ins with the captain.

Frank knew that Zimmerman wouldn't go out of his way to help a colored man. But then again, he was pretty sure he wouldn't go out of his way to hurt one either.

Two years ago, Zimmerman talked a vagrant out of jumping off the Brooklyn Bridge. Frank recalled he'd spent two hours talking him down and eventually got him off the edge.

Last year, he'd disarmed a drunken lunatic and stopped him from shooting his cheating girlfriend. Zimmerman talked to him for hours--standing on the sidewalk-- while the enraged man sat on his front porch waving a gun. Frank often wondered what would have happened if he had to calm down a colored man. Yeah, Zimmerman was real good at talking. But his prejudices always got in the way.

Weighing in at over two hundred fifty pounds, with a massive neck and burly body, he instilled fear in anyone daring to look into the eyes on his blotchy, red face. But Frank saw through the bullshit and knew him to be a big blowhard and nothing else. He was more than ready to challenge Zimmerman or anybody else who didn't feel Bobby John deserved a chance.

Chapter 4

ONE THING JOHNNY ZIMMERMAN KNEW for a fact was that whites belong with whites and coloreds belong with coloreds. His mama told him that as a boy, and his mama never lied, according to his recollection of things. She didn't have anything against Negroes; she just didn't want her family to have anything to do with them.

But it was a whole different story with Daddy, especially when he got to drinking. Johnny had walked home from school one day with a Negro boy who lived up the road from his family's farm. Daddy spotted his son with that colored boy and met him on the porch, a loaded rifle across his lap. When Johnny's friend spotted the gun pointed right at him, he stopped in his tracks and hightailed it back up the road to his house.

After putting the gun down, Mr. Zimmerman grabbed Johnny by his shirt collar and beat the tar out of him, right there in front of God and everybody. His daddy told him that he mustn't have anything to do with those niggers down the road. Johnny promised he wouldn't and that was the end of it. He was used to the beatings, and was just relieved that daddy hadn't shot his friend, being drunk and all.

* * *

Johnny Zimmerman left home at eighteen and hitchhiked across the country from Mississippi to New

York City with little money in his pocket and no food to speak of. It'd taken him just short of three weeks. His mama fixed him a meal of chicken and biscuits to take on the road, but that hadn't lasted long. She'd also put seven dollars in his pocket— money she'd been saving in a mason jar for a new wash tub.

He'd watched her crying on the front porch, as he walked down the dusty road toward the bus station at Missoula, hoping for a better life. Daddy had been passed out on the couch, and hadn't even said goodbye.

Johnny always knew he wanted to be a cop, and what better place than a big city like New York? After taking odd jobs to pay for a rented room and classes, he finished the course work at the police academy, and ended up at the Twentieth. He'd finally come to terms with his feelings about Negroes, and like his late mama, didn't want anything to do with them. And he was prepared to fight Kowalski all the way to make sure that Negro boy stayed away from his precinct.

Zimmerman got some support from the younger officers of the Thirty-Fourth, but only through harassment and intimidation—his only weapons. Although Johnny thought his sheer size ought to have scared the living hell out of most of them, even that strategy didn't play to his advantage.

Some of the veteran cops sided with him, but ultimately didn't want to anger Smallwood, whom they respected. In other words, they weren't ready for a fight.

So Zimmerman decided to go it alone. He told all of them they were a bunch of crying babies, and he didn't need their help. And since Bobby John Taylor didn't belong there, he was going to get rid of that colored boy on his own.

Chapter 5

FRANK ATE AND SMOKED TOO MUCH when he had a lot on his mind. And meeting Bobby John tomorrow night kept him tossing and turning all night long, with a bad case of heartburn to boot. He took a final drag on his cigarette and tossed it into the street. He was headed for Angelo's deli in Harlem because he was dying for a steak and cheese. Taking his chances in a bad neighborhood was worth it for the best food on the east side. But even though Harlem had its own problems, it also had its own cops.

Frank really didn't feel like a game of cops and robbers tonight, but when he looked into the window of Drake's liquor store, the look of sheer terror on the cashier's face stopped him cold. Frank looked to the backs of two Negro men. One of them pointed a snub-nosed revolver at the terrified man behind the counter.

He had no choice but to become involved.

Frank hadn't counted on a loud bell attached to the door, and it rang as he opened it, startling the would-be crooks. The man waving the gun spun around and fired twice—one bullet just missed his shoulder and one hit his leg above the knee. Frank didn't get a chance to fire a single shot. He dropped to the floor writhing in pain, clutching the leg of his blood-drenched pants.

Both thugs left the store and hit the streets running. The panic-stricken employee screamed for help, but the store was clearly empty.

Frank began to lose consciousness; his world moved in slow motion. He heard the bell again, but muffled this time. The screaming had stopped and he looked up to see a colored man in police uniform, removing his belt to use as a tourniquet. He tied it tightly around Frank's leg.

"Man, this is not your neighborhood, Detective. I'm guessing you just couldn't wait one more day to see me," Bobby John muttered.

Frank tried to focus on the familiar face leaning over him.

"Bobby John?"

"One and the same."

"I'm not dying, am I?" Frank whispered.

"Not if I can help it, Detective."

"I gotta tell you...so grateful. I only wanted steak and cheese." Frank's voice trailed off, his head cradled in Bobby John's lap. That was all he remembered of that night—the night that changed everything.

Chapter 6

FRANK WOKE UP WITH A SPLITTING HEADACHE. He'd already figured out he was in the hospital, but he was too groggy to remember how long he'd been there. The women in white had picked and poked at him all night, leaving him tired. A dim light shone through the window curtains, so he decided it must be morning. He turned his head to look and was startled to see Bobby John sitting in the chair next to his bed.

"How long have you been here?" he asked weakly.

"About an hour," Bobby John replied. "Just wanted to make sure you made it through another night. The captain stopped by after they brought you in, but they said you wasn't seeing visitors. He's been doing a lot of checking up on you. You didn't look so good when I found you—lost a whole lot of blood."

"How long have I been here?"

"Two days. They brought you in Friday night after you got shot. You remember anything?"

"Only that you showed up and promised me I wouldn't die."

"And I kept my promise. Been here every night since and I been doing a whole lot of thinking— sitting here all this time."

"About what?"

"Us maybe learning things from each other. Does that sound crazy, or what?"

"Yeah, but I'm used to crazy."

"So...I want something from you—when you're up to it, that is."

"Just name it and it's yours."

"I want you to teach me everything you know—about being a detective and all."

"You really serious?"

"I wouldn't be sitting here if I wasn't serious."

"And what are you going to teach me?"

"How to survive in Harlem without getting yourself shot. That oughta do for now."

"Only if you call me Frank. It just sounds right. And by the way, does this mean...?"

Bobby John cut him off. "It doesn't mean anything, Frank. I just want to learn from the best."

* * *

And so it began.

When Frank's leg started hurting, Bobby John made sure he got his pain medicine. When he got thirsty, B.J. lifted his head and gave him water. When Frank grew too tired to speak, he let him rest. Although the nurses didn't like it at first, they permitted the long visits because they felt their patient was getting stronger with this colored man's help.

Frank and Bobby John talked about everything from circumstantial evidence to physical evidence. They talked about fingerprints, shoe prints, hair and fiber evidence, as well as spent bullets and how to identify them. They discussed interrogation procedures, police protocol, keeping a clean crime scene, gathering evidence and how to process it once they had it.

On the fifth day, the day-shift nurse balked until Frank assured her he was up to it. But at four thirty P.M. she finally kicked Bobby John out of the room and pleaded with him to leave and come back tomorrow.

In what had become a ritual between the two, Bobby John leaned over the bed, shook Frank's hand, and told him to get some rest and that he would stop by again in the morning.

The night nurse gave him something for pain and tucked him in for the night with a warm blanket. His head was still hurting and his goddamn leg was killing him, but he felt good—really good. He could hardly wait until morning when he could see his friend again. They still had a helluva lot to talk about.

Frank soon drifted off to sleep.

Chapter 7

FRANK WOKE UP HUNGRY AS HELL and looking forward to breakfast. After five days in the hospital, he'd gotten used to hospital food, and it beat his cooking. A light knock sounded on his opened door. He looked up and saw Captain Smallwood standing in the doorway.

"Can I come in?" he asked.

"Are you kidding? Bobby John told me you've been keeping tabs on me."

"Yeah, the nurses seem real nice here. A little over-protective, but that's good, right?"

"We need to talk."

"About when you're coming back to work? Don't even worry yourself about it. Just get better. No hurry."

"I'm talking about taking Bobby John on as my partner."

"Frank, we've been over all this before. You can't really be serious about this?"

"Let me get this straight, for the record. You've been all over this before. I've had to listen to you tell me time and time again just how the whole damned world will be sorry if we let Bobby John come on board. He saved my life, Ron. That means a helluva lot to me. Look, he's been here every day. I'm teaching him all I know and he's ready. He'll be my responsibility."

Smallwood threw up his hands in exasperation, and dropped into the chair beside the bed. "Look, everybody in the precinct's talking about this, and Zimmerman's trying to get the entire force against Bobby John before he even takes the job."

"Damn Zimmerman. You're the boss. Why don't you act like one?"

Smallwood jumped up, banging his fist on Frank's tray table, fire in his eyes.

"And give you your goddamn way, like always—and screw everybody else!"

"That sounds about right."

"You are one stubborn son-of-a-bitch, Kowalski. You do know how much heat I'm going to take over this."

"It's the right thing to do."

"And just why do you think you're always right?"

"Maybe because I've never been wrong."

"Don't make me sorry I did this, Frankie. And for your information, he'll be my responsibility!"

Smallwood stormed out of the room, nearly knocking down the nurse carrying Frank's food tray.

Frank looked down at his eggs, toast and lukewarm coffee. To hell with it. He wasn't hungry after all.

Chapter 8

FRANK'S CRUISER WAS IN THE SHOP. Perfect timing. He stood on the deserted subway platform at five-thirty in the morning, waiting for the first train. It was a big day—officially Bobby John's first day with the Twentieth. Frank tossed and turned all night—questioning himself about the decision he'd made to make Bobby John his new partner. He could still hear Zimmerman's voice in his head: "I guess you don't get it Frankie. No colored boys wanted in this department."

He lit his first cigarette of the day, inhaling deeply, letting the smoke fill his lungs. Smoking was his only comfort lately, but something told him the damn things weren't good for him. Holding his thermos in one hand, he stepped into an almost empty train car. The lights above his head snapped and flickered as he took a seat.

It didn't take Frank long to realize that some things never change. A wino was passed out on a nearby seat, clutching an empty liquor bottle in a dirty paper bag. An old woman, carrying a purse, shot Frank a nervous glance. He wore a brown suit, and didn't think he looked dangerous. He thought he looked like a cop, but guessed she wasn't buying it. Frank straightened his tie, tipped his hat and attempted a weak smile. The train pulled into his station and came to a stop. The woman, holding her pocketbook even tighter to her chest, hurriedly left the train.

It was an early October morning with a chill in the air, as Frank walked briskly down the street, pulling his coat tightly around his neck.

Vendors were already setting up shop and proudly sweeping sidewalks in front of their stores. A neighborhood fruit and vegetable stand boasted brilliant red apples and the last of the season's succulent, vine-ripened tomatoes. The smell of sweet, fresh bread from Luigi's bakery made Frank realize how hungry he was. A freckle-faced boy in flannel leggings and a tam-o'-shanter hat, offered to shine his shoes for a nickel, but he waved him away.

A young boy in a tattered coat hawking *The New York Times* gave the officer a broad grin, and Frank tossed him a twenty- five cent piece for the paper. A quick glance of yesterday's news, showed no murders, rapes or botched drug deals. Come to think of it, Frank realized the past couple of days had been relatively quiet—petty larcenies, a bungled bank job and a few domestic disturbances. But it was early in the mean streets of New York—a new day. The lull before the frigging storm.

Frank loved the early morning—watching his city come to life. It gave him time to think before it got too crazy. He had the same routine every day, but it pleased him. After he got to the station, he would pour a large cup of coffee from his thermos—piping hot and strong— just like he liked it. Then, he'd spread out the paper on his desk, check out the Giants, and turn back to the front page to see what the city's criminals were up to.

Yesterday just happened to be a noteworthy day for newspapers around the world. Charles, "Lucky" Luciano, mobster kingpin, had been taken from prison and deported to Italy—never to walk on American soil again. It seemed after cooperating with the feds, they cut him a deal. Frank thought they ought to deport more of the bums, but that wasn't up to him.

Truth be told, some of N.Y.P.D.'s men were on the Mafia's payroll. It was easy money for dirty cops who thought they were above the law and could get away with it. Yeah, murder, mayhem and cops on the take. It was dirty business and Frank wanted no part of it.

This morning he entered the precinct station and walked into an almost empty squad room. He wandered over to his cluttered desk and made a feeble attempt to straighten it up. Dusting off the picture of his wife with his sleeve, he couldn't believe it had been almost two years since he lost her to cancer. Frank looked at the wall clock. It wasn't even seven A.M. His leg was killing him as usual, but the side effects of the painkillers were worse than the pain. It had been only six weeks since he'd been shot in the liquor store robbery gone bad, but he was anxious to get back to work. Smallwood thought he was coming back too early. Presumably his boss was worried about him, but Frank couldn't help thinking that the captain was just as happy not to deal with the new order of things in the station. He'd made that abundantly clear at the hospital. A welcoming committee for Bobby John sure as hell wasn't in the works, and Frank knew he had his work cut out for him.

* * *

Since Frank had been promoted before the shooting, he wasn't sure being a detective was such a big deal. Although not pleased about the whole situation, it would have made his wife happy. Yeah, she would have been real proud. Now, Frank had other things on his mind. Bobby John was supposed to report first thing in the morning.

Admittedly, no one wanted Bobby John here, especially as Frank's new partner. Zimmerman had already started a crusade to get rid of the "colored boy" before he even set foot in the station. Resentments were forming among the other officers and Frank knew they were talking about him behind his back. But to hell with all of them. Frank was adamant. Bobby John had saved his life and he wanted to repay him. He felt confident that his new friend was up to it; he'd been a beat cop for close to three years when they unofficially met at the "Y."

Just before eight A.M., Frank looked up to see Bobby John standing in front of his desk, nervously rattling the change in his pocket.

"Hope you don't mind sharing a desk until we get you settled," Frank said.

"No problem, Detective. I really didn't expect much more than a place to stand," Bobby John replied.

Frank, ignoring the stares from around the room, grabbed a chair, opened up his metal thermos and poured a cup of coffee for his new partner.

* * *

Three uneventful weeks went by. Bobby John finally got a beat-up desk from storage and things were relatively quiet among the ranks. After much consideration, Captain Smallwood conditionally promoted Bobby John to Detective Third Grade. The two of them had been working on a case in upper Manhattan involving a wealthy widow who was missing large sums of cash—all of it stashed in her apartment. It seemed the old gal didn't trust banks. Bobby John lifted two near perfect fingerprints from her bedroom dresser and they'd finally traced them to her dead-beat nephew down on his luck. He had one too many gambling debts and the mob was itching to collect. After mob goons broke one of his legs, he was ready for a confession. With Frank's help, Bobby John had gotten an arrest warrant and they apprehended the bum in a pool hall in Jersey. Bobby John had been tipped off by a snitch who owed him a favor. Life was looking good.

But Smallwood told Frank that he had another job for them— a big drug bust on Harlem's East side, Bobby John's old territory.

Chapter 9

JOHNNY ZIMMERMAN'S HUGE BODY cast a menacing shadow over Ron Smallwood's desk. The captain felt the anger rising up in his throat.

"In case I haven't already made myself perfectly clear, Zimmerman, this isn't a request. This is a direct order. I think we've already discussed the hell out of it."

"Yeah, I get it, Boss. But like I already told ya, I don't feel comfortable working with the coloreds. And there's plenty of officers out there who would jump at the chance to take down those slimy bastards on the East side. So, I'm just askin', why me?"

"And you think Bobby John feels 'comfortable' around any of you white guys; police officers who talk behind his back, telling nigger jokes— just waiting for him to slip up? It's even come to the point of downright disrespecting him and his badge. Just maybe because you need to get your head out of your ass for a moment and try—just try— to accept Frank's partner, instead of doing everything in your power to derail them."

"Nothing personal, Boss."

"Yeah, nothing personal. Right. I think it's all about 'personal,' and it's going to end right here, right now!"

Zimmerman turned around, and against his better judgment, stormed out of the office, slamming the door behind him.

Smallwood followed him and stuck his head out of the door.

"This is going down tomorrow night, Zimmerman, and in the future—don't slam my damned door!"

Several curious officers milled around Smallwood's office, trying to look busy.

"Any of you other gentlemen have a problem with the colored man, because there's a lot more Bobby John Taylor's out there, so you damn well better get used to it!"

Smallwood's anger was met with stone silence. He shot them a scowl and returned to his cluttered desk. He hated himself for losing his temper like that, but Zimmerman deserved what he got, and for that, he wasn't sorry.

The captain knew Bobby John had something to prove, and as God was his witness, Smallwood was going to do everything in his power to make it happen.

* * *

Just past midnight in a street with little foot traffic on Harlem's East side, the police-issued panel truck pulled up in front of a rundown row house. The truck was outfitted with the latest equipment—including a two-way radio and three walkie-talkies. Zimmerman sat behind the wheel.

It was a warm fall night, with people sitting on their stoops trying to catch a breeze. Despite the lateness of the hour, small kids laughed and played in front of their row houses, while the adults drank cheap beer and smoked cigarettes.

Two prostitutes, scantily dressed with painted faces, stood under a streetlight, drumming up business. Another had her head in the window of a blue sedan, negotiating a deal guaranteed to make one man's troubles go away, at least for a little while.

There had been little conversation between Frank, B.J. and Zimmerman on the way to the drug deal, but as the captain's man in charge, Frank finally spoke up.

"Let's go over this one more time. Bobby, you go inside to apartment Two A, ask for Mr. C., and show him a big wad of cash. Don't give him anything until he produces the dope. That's it. Signal us with your walkie-talkie and I'll head up to the apartment where we'll announce we're police officers and get access to the apartment—or kick in the door if we need to. Hopefully, we'll find more dope and make some arrests."

"In the meantime, I'll be watching the apartment, keeping my eyes peeled for anything suspicious."

"Zimmerman, you'll man the radio. If you hear anything fishy, or any gunfire, get your ass up to Two A for backup. But be careful. These bastards hate cops and wouldn't mind killing one, if they get a chance."

Bobby John walked up the two flights to apartment Two A, his heart pounding in his chest. The east side was his home turf, and he hoped he wouldn't be recognized before he pulled it off.

He knocked on the door, and after what seemed like an eternity, an unshaven colored man with a deep scar across his cheek, cautiously opened the door—just a sliver—and gave Bobby John the once over. The man opened it wider.

"You Mr. C?"

"Yeah. You got the cash?"

Bobby John flashed the large wad of bills in front of the greedy man. Instantly he put his arm out the door to grab it.

Bobby John took a step backward.

"No money until I see the stuff."

Mr. C. reached into his shirt pocket and pulled out a bag of white powder.

"Hand it over."

The colored man handed the heroin over to B.J., grabbed the cash and disappeared inside.

"Nice doin' business with ya," came from inside the apartment.

Bobby John was glad it was over. He turned to leave, but found two colored men standing on the landing.

"Looks like we got here just in time. We'd be happy to take that off your hands, mister. Mr. C.'s got plenty more where that came from, if you got the cash."

"I got no more cash," Bobby John said.

"Then I guess you're shit outa luck," said the first man, with a naked lady tattooed on his forearm.

The second man rushed Bobby, and wrestled him to the ground, pressing his boot against Bobby John's neck.

"He's armed!" yelled the first man. He began to check out Bobby's service revolver. B.J. struggled to get up.

"You don't think I'd be stupid enough to come alone to this neighborhood, do ya?"

"I don't see nobody comin' to help you out," the second man said.

"Would you look at that? He's a cop! Just look at the side of his pistol—N.Y.P.D.," proclaimed the tattooed man—the obvious leader of the two.

He pulled Bobby John to his feet, holding his pistol against Bobby John's head.

"I guess this just ain't your lucky day, Officer. Shot with your own weapon."

"Just do it, Boss, and let's get outa here," his nervous partner said.

"Two against one. That really doesn't seem fair, gentlemen, " a voice taunted from the entrance to the hallway.

Startled, the tattooed man turned and aimed the gun at Frank. B.J. reached for the gun and wrestled the man to the floor, all the while, struggling to get control of his revolver.

Waiting seconds to take a clean shot, Frank dropped to one knee, and fanned his weapon, emptying his service revolver into the bodies of the two thugs and mortally wounding them both.

Exhausted, Frank sank to the ground, bracing himself against the wall. Bobby John rushed to his side.

"Sweet Jesus, Frankie!"

"I'm too old for this crap, Bobby, but I knew you were in trouble when I saw those two bums going inside."

"So now we're even?"

"I certainly hope so."

Bobby John and Frank heard Zimmerman's heavy footsteps running up the stairs. Gun drawn, he was surprised to see them both sitting together on the floor, shaken up, but unharmed.

"What in the name of hell just went on up here?"

Zimmerman looked at the two bodies lying on the floor.

"Frankie figured out I was in trouble, and got here before my brothers over there blew my brains out."

"I couldn't have said it better myself."

"You two are made for each other," Zimmerman said with a wry grin.

Chapter 10

THE WOMAN SHRUGGED ON HER COAT, glanced at her watch and headed for a waiting cab. Though almost eight o'clock, her husband was still not home from the office. He would offer one of his usual excuses—a client needing help, paperwork that couldn't wait, or a late-night business meeting. She'd heard it all. She left a note saying she would be out to dinner with friends—not to wait up.

"Where to, miss?" the cabby asked.

"The San Moritz, please." The woman threw her black sable coat over her shoulder, as she climbed into the back seat.

She paid the driver when they arrived at her destination, then entered the lavish hotel lobby and headed for the bar. She knew who she was looking for, although she didn't know his name...yet. He had to be alone—a working professional from out of town—and married. She knew the type well. They were all equally loathsome. The only things she needed from him were a few cocktails and some polite conversation. It would only be a matter of time before he would succumb to her wiles and invite her up to his room for a nightcap.

She double-checked her purse for the chloral hydrate—concealed in a small, blue perfume bottle and adorned with a miniature glass swan. Her doctor had prescribed the drug for chronic insomnia, adding a stern warning against over-dosing. And he'd admonished her, never combine with alcohol—a potentially deadly mix. Not to worry, Doctor, she always replied.

She put on her most winsome smile and looked around for a suitable companion. She found two empty barstools, one with her name on it. Someone approached her from behind, his body brushing hers. Her face flushed.

"I promise to be absolutely charming if I may take this seat," uttered a tall, impeccably dressed man with a dazzling smile and a wedding band.

Perfect.

"And I promise to be absolutely charmed," she cooed. They slipped into casual conversation. Men were so gullible, and they toasted, in his words, "to a most unforgettable evening."

She'd already decided the night would be unforgettable.

"Forgive me. My name is Michael, Michael Bollinger. And you are…?"

"I'm afraid that will have to be my little secret," the woman whispered with a seductive smile.

Chapter 11

SHE HADN'T MEANT TO KILL HIM. After drinks at the bar, her plan had been to lure this perfect stranger back to his hotel room, lace his drink with the chloral hydrate concealed in her perfume bottle, and then leave him alone in his bed, unsatisfied and humiliated.

But Michael Bollinger had angered her from the beginning, with his arrogance and boasting of his countless infidelities. When he sat down on the bed, loosening his tie, she saw the effects of the drug-laced martini given only minutes before—slurred speech and droopy eyes. While he bragged about his last conquest and commented on his wife's stupidity, she calmly walked over to her sable coat draped over a chair. She reached deep into the pocket where she always carried a pair of white gloves.

He watched her in amusement as she put on the gloves and stood in front of him. Then he reached up and tried to pull her body on top of his, but she grabbed his necktie and tightened it with a ferocity that frightened her. She resisted his feeble attempts to grab her hands, as she roughly pushed down his arms. Her hatred toward this unwitting stranger consumed her, and she kept her hands firmly around his neck until the pain in her wrists became unbearable. Then she released her grip, and he slumped backwards onto the bed, obviously dead. She leaned over his body, stared into his lifeless eyes and felt for a pulse just to be sure. Nothing. She felt no remorse, nothing but relief. It was almost too easy, she thought to herself, as she lifted his legs, laid him down and folded his hands across his chest.

She cleaned up the room—wiping out the ashtray, and washing the martini glasses. Content that the room contained no hint of her presence, she picked up her coat and headed for the hotel lobby, where she took the elevator to the first floor and went outside to hail a cab. Noticing the chill in the October air, Sylvia wrapped her coat tightly around her neck. As she stepped into the taxi, she reached into her coat pocket, assuring herself that she had not forgotten her gloves.

On the ride home, she glanced at her watch. It was late. Her husband would be asleep. She gave a contrived smile to the driver—a sinister, swarthy man—who couldn't take his gaze off her. She knew Michael Bollinger would be found in the morning by a distraught maid and the police called. But as far as she was concerned, no crime had been committed. Mr. Bollinger had gotten just what he deserved.

* * *

Her mother was out of the country, tending to her ailing mother. She was only ten years old. Her father's legal secretary, Beatrice, was at the house working on a high profile case. She never liked the woman, an overly made-up floozy, with huge breasts and flame-red hair. She had come downstairs to ask cook for warm milk, when she heard muffled laughter coming from her father's study. Cautiously cracking open the door, not wanting to be seen, she saw Beatrice reclining on their satin sofa, blouse disheveled, her father's hand reaching up her skirt. Feeling both confused and angry, the young girl

Stranglehold

knew this was wrong. He wouldn't get away with this. She would make sure of it.

Chapter 12

FRANK WAS SOUND ASLEEP when the telephone rang. It was seven A.M. He'd overslept.

"Frank, I need you downtown, pronto," Smallwood said. "I don't want to go over the details over the phone."

"All right, give me a minute." Frank sat up and slowly swung his legs over the side of the bed, trying to wake up. The damned painkillers had left him groggy; he wished he hadn't even taken them.

"I'll be there, but…"

The phone went dead. What the hell? Frank hurriedly dressed, headed out the door and jumped in his cruiser. He was two blocks from the precinct when he spotted Bobby John standing on a street corner having a smoke. Frank rolled down the window of his squad car.

"What's up, Frank? You don't look so good," B.J. said.

"Get in. I got a wake-up call from Smallwood. Looks like trouble in paradise."

* * *

As soon as they entered the squad room, Smallwood intercepted them, ushered them into his office and shut the blinds.

He turned to face them, his expression somber. "You're not going to believe this."

"What is it?" Frank asked.

"Some big shot banker got himself killed at the San Moritz, and I've decided you're the best man for the job."

"Don't you mean I was the best?"

"No, dammit, you're still the best, but I'm having a little problem taking on a relatively new detective for this case."

Frank shot a glance at Bobby John, sensing his anger and frustration.

"B.J., would you mind stepping out into the hall for a minute?" Smallwood asked.

Bobby John walked out grudgingly, shutting the door behind him.

"Frank, you know you can take any man in this department. And you also know I'll back you on it; but taking Bobby John—I don't like it. Not one damn bit. What if something goes wrong? I take the blame for putting in the new guy—who, by the way—is a colored man and you go back to being a beat cop giving parking tickets."

"Bullshit. Nothing's going to go wrong. And Bobby John being a negro has nothing to do with it. Maybe you're just scared of what people will say."

Smallwood's face reddened. "Maybe I am."

"Sorry, it's Bobby John or count me out. Look, he's got good instincts, and he can chase leads with the best of 'em. Besides that, we trust each other and we're just getting started."

Bobby John opened the door and entered the room, breaking the conversation.

Smallwood had little choice and no time to argue the point.

"You two going, or maybe I should change my mind?" he snapped.

"We're going Captain. Don't you worry. We can handle it," Bobby John said.

Frank slapped Smallwood on the back and followed his partner out of the station.

Smallwood hoped he wasn't making a big mistake, but something told him taking Bobby John was going to be the least of his worries.

Frank and Bobby John drove into Manhattan's Central Park South and managed to park less than one block from the grand San Moritz Hotel.

"This place is mobbed," muttered Bobby John, looking at the luxury hotel looming in front of them. Though only nine in the morning, the place already crawled with police and reporters. When they got to the top of the outside stairway, Bobby John stopped, and with an incredulous look on his face, said, "Frankie, this is big—really big."

Frank only nodded in agreement. He didn't need anybody telling him this was big. His palms sweated, his head pounded and his bum leg throbbed like a sonofabitch. He prayed he was up to it.

The obviously young rookie guarding the entrance to the hotel stepped in front of them. "Hey, this is a crime scene here."

"Detective Kowalski from the Two-Zero, and my partner, Detective Taylor," Frank said as they flashed their badges. The inexperienced cop looked contemptuously at Bobby John, but stepped aside and waved them both on.

"Sorry. Go right up. Eighth floor, room eight ten."

Frank and B.J. took the elevator to the eighth floor, then entered the room, and made their way to the small mob encircling the bed.

* * *

Sam Giordano, N.Y.P.D.'s Chief Medical Examiner, turned towards them and grinned. "Hey, Frankie, I heard you been real busy fixing parking tickets!"

Bobby John was getting ready to come to his friend's defense, when he sensed the familiarity between them. Giordano offered B.J. a firm handshake. "Welcome aboard. Any friend of Frankie's is a friend of mine." Bobby John smiled suspiciously at the short, fat man with the black, curly hair.

"Always a practical joker," Frank said. "Whadaya got for us, Sammy?"

"Looks like he's from out of town—Michael Bollinger—investment banker from Chicago and married. And get this: his wife was in town on personal business—staying with old college friends. Cause of death: apparent strangulation—by his own tie—for Chrissakes. Body's basically untouched; no bruising, trauma. Looks to me like he died before the fun. My boys checked out the two empty martini glasses on the bedside table. They were wiped clean. According to them, there were no prints— not even on the doorknobs. My best guess would establish time of death at approximately midnight. Maid found him this morning when she came to clean the room. She says she didn't touch anything. The front desk called police."

Frank's eyes were drawn to the man on the bed. Except for the obvious swelling around the neck, he looked like he was sleeping. He was lying down, hands neatly folded across his chest, his suit immaculate. He still had his shoes on. The poor bastard didn't even know what hit him.

"Sammy, have the lab check out what the victim ate and drank last night," Frank said. "Also, I'd like to talk to the wife later. Send her over, will ya? I'm taking

Bobby John over to the lab to go over anything your boys find."

"Will do, Frankie. Really nice working with you again. You too, Bobby John," Giordano said with a broad grin.

"Let me know if you find anything else for me," Frank said.

"You'll be the first to know," promised Sam.

* * *

Just as Sam predicted, time of death was officially established around twelve o'clock midnight. Frank had dropped B.J. off at the crime lab and was back at the station when he received a call from his partner early in the afternoon.

"Not much to go on, Frank. The lab couldn't find anything in the glasses. But there were black hairs taken from one of the chairs that look like fur from a coat—most likely—a woman's coat. But I got a question for you. Just how could a man this guy's size—about one hundred seventy pounds and six foot two—be strangled by a lady without any kind of a fight? You got a good look at him. Looked like he'd been takin' a nap."

"I'm thinking Bollinger might have been unconscious before he was strangled. Get my drift?"

"Frank, you're a friggin' genius."

Chapter 13

FRANK SAT AT HIS DESK, establishing a timeline for the Moritz Hotel job, when Smallwood approached him, accompanied by a tall brunette with a killer body and ruby red lips just begging to be kissed.

Frank tried to get a quick take on the woman standing in front of him. Smallwood pulled up a chair and offered it to the recent widow. She sat down and folded her delicate hands on her lap. She appeared surprisingly composed, eyes devoid of emotion.

"Detective Kowalski, this is Mrs. Bollinger, wife of the deceased, Michael Bollinger," offered a somber Smallwood before hastily retreating to his office.

"Good afternoon, Mrs. Bollinger. I'm so sorry for your loss. It must be quite a shock."

"On the contrary, Detective, my husband's untimely demise doesn't surprise me in the least. He was always out of town on business, always with another woman, but had always returned to his dutiful wife. It looks like this time he made a rather unfortunate choice. I've made my statement to Captain Smallwood. If there are no more questions, I do need to get back home to make the necessary arrangements."

"Sounds like you shared your life with a real Casanova."

"Detective, the only things I 'shared' with this man were our physical residence and our name. I shed my last tears for him a lifetime ago. Now, if you'll excuse me." Mrs. Bollinger abruptly got up, revealing long, slender legs, and walked away without looking back.

"I will be calling you to answer a few more questions," Frank blurted out, as she disappeared down the hall. He hoped she had a good alibi. Suddenly, the woman with the killer body began to look like the woman with the killer motive.

Frank got up and paced in front of his desk. If this broad didn't have a decent alibi and an even better lawyer, this case might be closed before it was opened. Just as he suspected, it was probably another jealous wife killing her husband after years of abuse and infidelity. Frank sat down and poured himself another cup of coffee, trying to imagine that body in a prison uniform. When the phone rang, he almost jumped out of his chair.

"Frankie, it's me, Sammy. Looks like someone slipped our friend—Mr. Bollinger—a 'mickey.' Not enough to kill him, but mixed with the martinis, enough to make him give up the fight. And Mrs. B. has an airtight alibi—attending a cocktail party here in the city with four close friends the night of the murder. And they're ready to testify to the fact."

"Sammy, you're killing me! What the hell was in the drink?"

"Chloral hydrate, my friend; better known on the street as 'knock-out drops.'

"Looks like the heartless wife is off the hook," muttered Frank in disbelief.

Chapter 14

BOBBY JOHN TAYLOR VOWED to get out of the rat-hole he'd been living in alone since his wife left eight months ago. He wearily climbed the three flights to the tenement apartment he shared with a stray cat. Bobby heard the usual noises as he turned the key to his place—crying babies, screaming mothers and rats scurrying down an empty stairwell.

He went to the refrigerator for a cold beer and fell into the one easy chair furnishing his sparse apartment. It still showed signs of children living there—a broken bookshelf holding a kid's book, a small toy car and a puzzle missing most of its pieces--things left behind when Beverly split with his two kids and most of the furniture. He missed his kids. Hell, he even missed his wife, but she just didn't understand.

Bobby John had never stopped dreaming of solving the big case, and for a colored police officer in New York City, it seemed all but impossible. But he knew Frank could make it happen. He was a good man, an honest man, and in a white man's world, Frank Kowalski was one of the best. Taught him everything he knew from a hospital bed.

Solving the rich old lady's case in upper Manhattan was just the beginning. Now, the Moritz homicide brought the new partners even closer together, and left Bobby John hungry for more. Although he hadn't mentioned it to Frank, he had a bad feeling this murder wouldn't be the last, but he planned to keep that to himself for the time being.

Making Smallwood happy would take more time. The conditional promotion was the first step, but Bobby John knew enough to take things slow. That meant working a little harder, a little longer, knowing his place, and keeping his mouth shut. Damn—that was the hard part. Shooting off his mouth came natural, almost like breathing. But solving the Moritz murder just might do the trick and make Smallwood finally believe in him.

* * *

Bobby John suddenly realized how tired he was. He stood and headed for the bedroom, taking his clothes off along the way. The unending fight coming from the next apartment became too much for him to bear. He pounded on the wall for some relief, screaming, "Shut the hell up or I'll shut you up for good!" Things managed to quiet down, and after drinking a second beer, he drifted off into a troubled sleep.

Bobby woke early to the sounds of sirens outside his bedroom window. He got dressed, fixed himself something to eat, fed the cat and headed off to the station before six o'clock. Last week, one of his snitches told him about his cousin, Dwayne, who'd been brought in for questioning for beating up his old lady. Shit, some things never change. But even at his lowest moment, Bobby never even thought about hitting a woman. That just wasn't right. Maybe that's why I do what I do. People need protecting.

Chapter 15

RIDDING THE WORLD OF SCUM. That was Ron Smallwood's philosophy when he was a rookie over fifteen years ago. He'd arrested his fair share of petty thieves, bank robbers and sleazy drug dealers. But he rose to the top five years ago with the arrest and conviction of a well-publicized child murderer and soon became one of N.Y.P.D.'s most respected police captains.

Now, Smallwood headed home to Brooklyn. It'd been a long night at the San Moritz, combing room eight ten for any evidence at a most disturbing crime scene. Sweet Jesus. Strangled by his own tie.

He pulled his unmarked cruiser into the driveway, got out, and entered the house. His wife, Ann, had left a table lamp on for him. It was late—very late. Smallwood hoped his wife was sleeping. He quietly undressed and slipped into bed, trying not to wake her. She woke, with a sleepy, "What time is it?"

"Two –thirty, and I hope I can sleep."

Smallwood had called his wife earlier, telling her he'd be late. He'd filled her in on some of the details, but for good reason, failed to mention anything about Frank and Bobby John.

"So…who's working the case?"

"Frank—and get this, he said he wouldn't take it on unless Bobby John works it with him."

"That's pretty understandable, Ronnie. Frank's been ready to get back to work and they've been a team for well over a month now."

"For God's sake, Annie, that colored boy might not be up to this job. Frank's defending him like he's his own goddamn son! Look, a banker from out of town gets killed in my city and I can't afford to mess it up!"

"Ronnie, Bobby's good. You even said so. Just give him a chance. All he needs is a chance." She spoke softly and turned her warm body toward his.

"How'd you get to be so smart?" Smallwood gently touched her face, closed his eyes, and tried to shut out the day.

Chapter 16

RODNEY DAVIS POSED A REAL PROBLEM. She knew she had to act quickly, have him take the bait, and get the man back to his room before he was too drunk to stand up. Mr. Davis reeked of alcohol when he first made a pass at her at The Plaza Hotel bar. She saw a gold wedding band on his plump finger and decided to make him her next conquest.

Her feigned interest in his life as a high-powered attorney repulsed her, but he proved to be a quick study. Within an hour, he stumbled to the elevator and she helped him back to his room

Once inside, the woman walked over to the bed and instructed him to sit down. She promised a cold drink, but that was all. Rodney Davis gave a hearty laugh and roughly pulled her to his chest. The stench of alcohol on his breath drove her mad with rage. When she looked into his bloodshot eyes, she only saw her father. This wouldn't be a difficult decision at all. She had to kill him. It would be no accident this time. She would feel no remorse, no pity, for this man.

* * *

Her father leaned over her, kissing her neck. She smelled the alcohol on his breath and pretended to be asleep. He ran his finger across her breasts and lifted her gown, touching her thighs. She was only twelve years old. She prayed that he wouldn't notice her body trembling while he repeated this perverse ritual night after night. When he left her room, he always whispered in her ear that if she told anyone, he would kill her, and she hated him for it. But the night her father died, she got away with murder, and no one, not even her mother, shed a single tear. Killing him over and over again in her mind was the only thing that consoled her. And damn her mother to hell—she who knew every sordid detail of her husband's abuse—crying quietly outside her room--too frightened to speak.

Chapter 17

MAYBE IT WAS ALL THE COFFEE, but Frank hadn't been able to sleep worth a damn since the Bollinger homicide. It had been close to two weeks, and still no leads. He and Bobby John had gone over the crime scene once again looking for any evidence that was missed the first time. Hair, supposedly from a fur coat, had already been submitted to the lab, but the case was at a complete standstill. Late Saturday afternoon, Smallwood told them both to go home, get some sleep, and he would see them first thing Monday morning.

Bobby John headed off to his Uncle Louis's house for a home-cooked meal.

Frank really needed a good night's sleep, so he drove to a ribs joint, where he polished off a plate of ribs and looked forward to climbing into a warm bed when he got home.

Frank switched on the light and entered his small living room. Frank muttered that the house sorely needed a woman's touch. Newspapers were scattered on furniture, clothes carelessly draped over chairs, and dirty dishes piled high on the coffee table. Frank had made a promise to himself to get the house cleaned up when he had the chance, but excuses came easy. Living alone wasn't.

Things in the house hadn't changed much since Alice died. He liked it that way. It was as if she never left, but who was he kidding? Glassware and trinkets, treasures his wife stubbornly clung to, filled a corner china cabinet. The worn, lace tablecloth still covered the dining room table, where family and friends had once gathered for family holidays.

Alice's easy chair sat across from his, a wicker basket next to it, filled with knitting needles, yarn and projects not completed. He eased himself into her chair, closed his eyes and tried to feel her presence. He realized she was slowly slipping away and this saddened him. He tried to read an old magazine tucked into the side of her chair, but he was too tired to concentrate. He ambled up the stairs to their bedroom, rubbing his leg. The tiny room with its pink chintz draperies and flowered wallpaper didn't suit him, but comforted him at the same time.

Frank worried about his leg. He hoped he was up to finishing this case—if there was a finish. Maybe it would go down as another unsolved murder and the case would eventually go cold. As much as he hated to admit it, maybe Michael Bollinger was a real son-of-a-bitch and deserved it.

Around nine o'clock, against his better judgment, Frank took the telephone off the hook. He was sick and tired of the damn phone always ringing. He fell into bed with his clothes on and drifted into a deep sleep. The sound of a distant siren woke him and he sat up with a start. He put the phone back on the hook and had no sooner laid back down, when the telephone rang. Frank fumbled for the phone, squinting into the face of his alarm clock. He sat up and turned on the bedside lamp.

"Frank, it's me. I've been trying to get a hold of you all night. Your damn phone's been busy for hours. Are you sleeping?"

Frank recognized Smallwood's voice.

"Am I sleeping? This had better be good. It's four in the goddamn morning!"

"She's got another one, Frank. Plaza Hotel. Same M.O. Apparently, a female called for room service at midnight. The busboy came in around twelve fifteen and found the room empty, except for a dead body with his neck in a noose. Nothing's been touched. Giordano and his boys are on their way."

Frank listened in silence, dumfounded. How could this be happening? It was supposed to be an isolated crime, a onetime event, a cheating husband murdered by his jealous wife or an angry girlfriend.

"Be there as soon as I can."

Two blocks from the precinct station, Frank took a detour to the Mansfield Hotel. He needed to talk to Melvin, the doorman— Bobby John's friend and snitch. Melvin was already in place, standing under the awning of the famous hotel. He recognized Frank and smiled.

Frank wound down his window and leaned out.

"Melvin, you need to do me a big favor. If you see Bobby John, tell him to meet me at The Plaza Hotel right away. Can you do it?"

Melvin nodded. "Some kinda big crime goin' down, right?"

"Yeah, you could say that."

"No problem."

"Thanks." Frank drove off.

Smallwood had sounded pretty damn scared on the phone. Frank felt pretty damn scared himself. He felt that familiar pounding in his chest and his head was starting to hurt. His aching leg was the least of his problems.

Around six A.M., Frank parked his cruiser and walked up to the entrance of The Plaza. Melvin hadn't disappointed him. He found Bobby John waiting on the steps.

"Bobby," Frank said, "it looks like we got a serial killer on the loose, and this dame's not wasting any time."

"She got another one?" asked an incredulous Bobby John.

"Yeah, another sap falling for a convincing broad who had other things on her mind."

"Like finishing him off."

They proceeded up the hotel steps, only to be greeted by a swarm of reporters, hot after a story; especially after the homicide at the San Moritz less than a month ago. Reporters hounded them with questions as they pushed their way through the lobby.

"Detective, any leads in the Bollinger murder?"

"Any connection between the Moritz murder and the one last night?"

"Detective, was the latest victim from out of town? Was he married? Has his family been notified?"

"No comment, boys. Now, if you'll excuse us." Frank and Bobby John hurried to a waiting elevator, where an officer directed them to the seventh floor.

Sam Giordano met them at the door, a look of grave concern on his unshaven face. Frank thought his friend looked ten years since murder number one. Smallwood was barking orders at one of Sam's boys, and thankfully hadn't seen Frank and B.J. enter the room. Sam led them to the bed.

"Take a look for yourself, fellas. Looks like our little lady found herself another chump. Married lawyer from Washington, D.C. Identified as one Rodney Davis. It seems he was here on business, defending some guy in a capital murder case."

Mr. Davis lay on the bed, arms folded across his chest, dressed in a very expensive suit and very dead. His tie was tightly secured around a bloated neck, and like Bollinger, still wore his shoes.

"Frankie, this broad's doing a real number on us," Sam groaned.

"Yeah, and she's doing a pretty damn good job of it," Frank retorted.

"Nothing in the martini glasses?' Bobby John asked Sam. As before, two empty glasses sat on the bedside table.

"No... nothing. And not a print in the whole goddamn place. No one saw Davis in the hotel bar and no one saw a man of his description leave with a woman. My men questioned the bartender and are talking to all the regulars. Nobody saw nothing."

Frank got close and studied the body. What would drive a woman to do this, not once, but twice? Someone with a grudge, no conscience or a man-hater. He knew the type. He'd even jailed a few. Frank knew they had to find her before it was too late. Hell, it was already too late, and Smallwood wasn't going to cut them any slack this time.

Captain Smallwood walked over to the bed, shaking his head in exasperation. "We're starting to look bad, really bad, Frank. This dame's got us by the balls and she's tightening her grip. All we know for sure is that both victims were unconscious before they were strangled. Chloral hydrate was found in Bollinger's body, and I'm pretty damned sure it'll be in Davis' body. So we need to ask ourselves; who in the name of living hell is this woman? What's her motive? Maybe she's just playing with us, but I'm beginning to think we haven't heard the last of her. Jesus, Frank, we need to stop this insanity before the commissioner calls for all our resignations." Smallwood slumped into an easy chair next to the corpse, rubbing his forehead in exasperation.

"Sam thinks we ought to call Violet," Frank said without hesitation.

"You mean that hooker from the Bronx that helped us with the Smithson case?"

"Yeah, one and the same. The St. Regis isn't far from The Plaza. I think the killer's smart enough not to hit the same place twice. Suppose we pay Violet to hang around the hotel bar and look for our lady, snuggling up to some unsuspecting sucker. She could give us a description—something to go on."

Sam quickly added, "She's good, Ron, and I understand she's taking a real liking to Frank."

"Frank really is good with the ladies, Boss," Bobby John said with a grin.

"Is that so?" Smallwood nodded. "I guess we have nothing to lose. Call her, Frank, and set it up."

Smallwood remembered he had a late morning meeting with Commissioner Delgado. He would assure him that his team was on top of things. He wouldn't even mention using Violet as a decoy to trap the killer—not yet, anyway. Smallwood only hoped he'd sound convincing, because he was having trouble convincing himself. He took a final look at Davis's body before Giordano's men started bagging it for the trip to the morgue. He made a promise to himself this would be the last victim. This dame was smart, but he wasn't about to be outwitted again, especially by a woman.

Chapter 18

VIOLET SAT AT HER DRESSING TABLE and stared at herself in the mirror. It had been a long day, with no prospective clients. "Mirrors don't lie. I still got what it takes, boys. Just take a number and stand in line." She laughed out loud, and began to carefully take off her old makeup. Business had been slow. Except for being an occasional snitch for the cops, she couldn't stay busy even four nights a week.

She looked closely at her pouty red lips and almost translucent skin. Her face, although still beautiful, was beginning to fade. Maybe she should consider taking an honest job. Nah, who was she kidding? She enjoyed the risk and she loved the attention—and the money wasn't bad either. Yeah, she was still a show-stopper— no doubt about it.

She was about to dress for the evening when the phone rang.

"Hey doll face, it's Frank. How about making a little extra cash?"

"I been real busy lately, honey, but I always got time for my favorite man in blue," Violet cooed.

"Can you meet me at Duffy's—say about seven?"

"Can't wait, gorgeous."

* * *

Stranglehold

When she arrived at Duffy's bar, a seedy joint in lower Manhattan, she found it already crowded. The music was loud and the rooms were smoky, but the drinks were cheap. She spied Frank scanning the bar, looking for his trusted informant.

She snaked an arm around his waist. He turned and put his arm around her, and led her to an empty booth in the back.

"Sit down, sweetheart. I'm about to cut you a really sweet deal."

Violet fluttered those warm, wet eyes, and slipped into the booth next to him.

"Start talking baby, 'cause I'm listening."

Chapter 19

VIOLET ARRIVED AT THE ST. REGIS HOTEL and entered the bar around ten. She felt comfortable knowing Frank waited in the hotel lobby. If she saw anything at all suspicious, she was to grab him and follow the unsuspecting couple to the elevator and up to their floor. Frank would take over from there. After that, she was supposed to make herself scarce.

She ordered her usual Manhattan and sat alone at the end of the bar. She'd hit The Carlyle last night, but with no action. Tonight promised to be another big waste of time, but she owed Frank a favor, and she wasn't about to welch. She'd always liked the Regis and asked herself why she'd stayed away so long. The crowd was fast and there was usually a fair share of paying customers. Two previous hotel murders hadn't dampened anyone's spirits; the place was packed.

One of the regulars was about to order Violet another drink, when she saw a tall blonde in a black sable coat sitting at the opposite end of the bar. Twenty minutes later, after a brief introduction, a very attractive man sat beside her.

Violet told her friend, Mack, to 'beat it,' that she was on a job, but he wouldn't take no for an answer.

"I told ya; I ain't working tonight, honey."

"I won't bother you none, Vi. I just hate drinking alone."

"Suit yourself, but like I told ya…"

Close to midnight, Violet, having had enough of Mack, decided to freshen up in the powder room and then report back to Frank that her lady appeared to be just another lonely woman drinking with a very handsome man.

She returned shortly after, and thankfully found Mack gone, but her seat had been taken. Her gaze shot to the other end of the bar, and her heart sank when she realized the couple she was tailing had gone. She pushed her way through the crowd, and got the attention of the bartender.

"Jake, did you happen to see that blonde at the end of the bar leave with a guy a couple of minutes ago?"

"Vi, honey, I don't make a habit of checking who comes and goes. I just serve the paying customers, which brings me to your bill—two dollars and seventy five cents. Your friend stiffed you for the last two drinks before he split."

"Jake, you don't understand. I just mighta cost some schmuck his life."

"Whadaya talking about, baby?"

"That man with the blonde you been serving; he just might be tomorrow's front page news. That's what I'm talking about!"

Jake shot her a puzzled look. She threw a five dollar bill on the counter and ran out of the bar. She didn't have the guts to talk to Frank. She had to gather up the courage to call him, or maybe she should tell him in person. In any case, it would have to wait until morning, so she could get her story straight. Maybe she was imagining the worst, anyway. No need to alarm Frankie for no good reason. Besides, they looked like just another couple looking for love.

Violet headed for the lobby, fully prepared to sneak out, when she spotted Frank. Oh God, he was actually sleeping in a chair, eyes closed, a magazine clutched in his hands. He must have gotten tired of waiting. Her conscience got the best of her and she slipped out the front door where she hailed a cab and headed for Duffy's. She quickly made her way to the back of the bar to a payphone and reached for a crumpled phone number in the bottom of her purse.

"Captain Smallwood, it's Violet…Violet Zussman." I've got some important information for you. Can you meet me at Duffy's, say in about an hour?"

"It's pretty late, Miss Zussman, but yeah, I'll be there. Get a table in the back. And Violet—this had better be good." Smallwood hung up.

* * *

Smallwood arrived late and spotted Violet sitting at a secluded booth, away from the usual crowd of late-night pool hustlers and rowdy drunks. Bing Crosby could be heard crooning one of Violet's favorite tunes from the jukebox in the corner.

He took a seat next to her, noting that she looked upset. An unenthusiastic bartender brought them a couple of stale coffees and told them the bar was about to close.

"I think I mighta' messed up tonight, Captain," Violet confessed. "I was watching a couple in the bar at The Regis for a couple of hours. Around midnight, I left for a minute to freshen up in the lady's room. When I came back, they were gone…split. Probably just a couple of strangers meeting over drinks, right?"

Smallwood tried to appear calm, but he felt a sense of dread he couldn't shake. "Maybe it was just a chance encounter and it was all perfectly harmless."

Violet smiled. "That's what I was thinking."

"Or maybe it was a guy thinking he was about to get lucky, and a woman who was only thinking about slipping a noose around the poor bastard's neck after slipping him a mickey!"

Violet looked at Smallwood in horror. "No sir, I'm sure that's not it at all."

"Right... and just where was Frank during all this?"

Violet didn't want to snitch on her friend, but Smallwood's intense stare finally got the best of her. "He was in the lobby, just as we planned, sitting by the fireplace. Taking a little nap, if I recall."

"Is that so? All that waiting must have worn him out," Smallwood said with a sneer. Wearily, the captain got up. "I'll be in touch, Miss Zussman." He thanked her for her time, slipped a five dollar bill on the table, and headed for home.

* * *

It had been a long night, but Violet decided to go back to the Regis for a couple of drinks. It seemed like a friendly crowd, and she wasn't ready to go home. She made a promise to herself to call Frankie in the morning. She found an empty barstool, and sipped another Manhattan. Violet wondered if she was even going to get paid for her trouble—especially since things hadn't gone as planned.

* * *

Smallwood drove down his empty street at close to three in the morning. He had an uneasy feeling that wouldn't go away, and the lousy coffee at Duffy's made him jittery. He should've had that bourbon when he'd had the chance. He planned to make himself a strong one when he got in the house. It looked like Violet apparently did her job, but Frank had a lot of explaining to do--sleeping on the damned job.

Before the call from Violet, he'd decided to go to bed early. Ann was visiting her mother in the country, and he needed some rest. A stiff drink and a good book. That was the plan, but Violet sure as hell screwed that up.

Smallwood finished his drink and went to bed, and had an unsettling sleep. In his dreams, he was the next victim, struggling to free himself from the noose, while a woman stood in the shadows, smiling at him with satisfaction.

Chapter 20

FRANK WOKE WITH A SPLITTING HEADACHE and a bad feeling about how things went down last night. After he'd left Violet in the lobby of the St. Regis, he wandered around the hotel for over an hour, hoping Violet was going to track down the killer who was beginning to make his department look like a bunch of blithering idiots.

He must have fallen asleep in a chair in the lobby, when he awoke with a start and looked at the clock over the front desk. It was almost one in the morning and he guessed Violet had split. He couldn't blame her. She'd checked out The Carlyle the night before, with no luck and felt she was wasting her precious time.

Frank checked the bar, confirming that she'd already left, then headed for home. He planned to call Violet in the morning.

Now he and Bobby John had an early morning meeting with the captain to discuss evidence found at the Rodney Davis crime scene—evidence that hopefully would get them back into Smallwood's good graces.

The previous day, Frank and Bobby John had returned to the Plaza to see if anything had been missed. Bobby John had managed to lift a muddied left shoeprint from a woman's high-heeled shoe at the marbled entrance to Davis's hotel room. He also found several more black fibers on a chair that were consistent with those found at the Bollinger murder scene.

Frank and Bobby John headed straight for Frank's desk to pour some strong coffees from his trusty thermos, and were surprised to see a bleary-eyed Smallwood sitting in Frank's chair, nervously tapping his pencil.

Bobby John frowned. "What's up, Boss?"

"You wanna know what's up? I'll tell you what's up. We got Thomas Douglas, real estate broker, married, from Seattle, dead in his bed at the St. Regis, with a noose around his neck! Sound familiar, boys? I got a call from the commissioner's office this morning, filling me in on all the grisly details."

Frank and Bobby John looked at Smallwood in disbelief.

Frank finally spoke up. "What about Violet? We were at the St. Regis last night!"

"Yeah, I already know the two of you were there. She gave me a late night call. It seems Violet left to powder her nose around midnight, and when she came back from the ladies room, the couple she'd been tailing were long gone. And correct me if I'm wrong, Frank; you were sleeping like a baby in the lobby when Violet decided to leave without even telling you—that crazy broad! The press is going to have a field day with this one, gentlemen. And Frank, if you think for one minute we're going to pay this hooker for her very costly mistake, you got another thing coming! She's off the case for good—no discussion. Trusting a snitch to crack this big a case—I must have been out of my goddamn mind!"

Frank felt mad as hell with Violet, but he wanted to hear her side of the story. Talking to Violet would have to wait, though. He and Bobby John were headed off to yet another crime scene.

"And don't come back until you got something—hear me? I'm due at Delgado's office for my own private lynching!" Smallwood yelled, and stormed out of the station.

* * *

Room nine hundred and one of the St. Regis wasn't any different from the others. The third victim, Thomas Douglas, was lying down in the bed, flawless, in a three-piece suit. His necktie was secured tightly around a visibly purple neck. Shoes on.

Sam Giordano wasn't making any jokes this time. He sat in a chair by the window with his head in his hands. Frank approached his friend, and laid a hand on his shoulder.

"We got nothing,' Frank…nothing," Sam whined.

With a feeling of helplessness, Bobby looked into the troubled eyes of his partner and walked over to the nightstand. Two martini glasses had been wiped clean, as well as a small crystal ashtray. He glanced down at the richly carpeted floor and spotted something next to the bed. He kneeled down to get a closer look.

"Hey, Frankie, looks like she left somethin' for us." With gloved hands, he carefully picked up one spent match that had been torn from a matchbook, and placed it in an evidence bag. "I think she slipped up this time. Now all we gotta do is find the missing matchbook—maybe with the hotel's name on it."

"Yeah—and how in the hell are we going to do that? It's just one goddamn match!"

"It's somethin,' Frankie—something to go on," Bobby John insisted.

"He's right Frank. The dame's finally getting sloppy, starting to show her hand," Sam quipped. Mistakes like this just might prove to be her undoing, boys. Good job, Bobby John."

But to Frank, it was like falling into a deep, dark hole, with no way out. He'd vowed that the second murder would be the last, but things had gone horribly wrong. As for falling asleep on the job—damn—there was no excuse. And for trusting Violet with such a crucial case, he only blamed himself.

Frank walked to to the bed and stood over the lifeless body. "Sam, have the lab check Mr. Douglas for chloral hydrate." He knew he was starting to sound like a broken record, and he sensed Sam felt the same way.

"Sure thing. And Frank, don't worry. We're gonna nail this bitch."

Chapter 21

AT AGE THIRTY, JEREMY FISCHER HAD A BRIGHT FUTURE in the real estate business. His firm was sending him to New York, hoping to snag a perspective client. This was his first business trip and his new bride was reluctant to see him go, but was finally convinced by her loving husband.

Jeremy rang for room service after he checked into the Waldorf Astoria at approximately seven P.M. He ate a light dinner in his suite overlooking the city's skyline, but soon tired of staying in his room. He decided to head down to the hotel bar for a drink, after calling home to say he arrived safely.

* * *

The woman's husband was out of town for the second time in less than a month. She felt unusually restless and needed a man to amuse her for the evening, so she decided to leave the house and get a room for the night. She called for a cab, arrived at the Waldorf at eight P.M. and checked into her room to freshen up. She headed for the bar earlier than usual, and took a seat at the far end of the bar. Usually she didn't look at younger men, but the boyish good looks of the man sitting two bar stools down attracted her. The woman smiled. He would be easy to seduce.

After a brief introduction and a couple of drinks, she had no difficulty in getting Jeremy Fischer to go back to his room for a nightcap. He leaned on her shoulder for support, as they headed up to his suite. When they entered the room, everything changed.

Jeremy walked over to the bed, sat down, and kicked off his shoes. That wasn't part of the plan. She started to panic, but regained her composure after she quickly laced his drink.

His sobs drew her attention back to the man on the bed.

* * *

"I can't do this. I really can't," he said through his tears. "I'm married and I love my wife. It's wrong and I'm so sorry. I didn't mean for things to go this far. If I could trouble you for a glass of water, you'll need to leave."

Jeremy reached for the glass with the lethal drink, but she deliberately blocked his hand with hers and the glass tumbled to the floor.

"I'll leave," the shaken woman said. "You're right; this isn't going to work."

He led her to the door. She stepped into the empty hallway, and much to his relief, disappeared from view.

She entered her room, lay down on the bed and began to cry uncontrollably, clutching a pillow for comfort. Despite troubling thoughts running through her head, she eventually fell asleep. She began to dream.

The little girl gathered pebbles by the pond in the back of her house. She was only five years old and not allowed to go near it, but a smooth stone caught her eye. She reached into the shallow water to grab it, lost her balance and toppled into the water. Her leg caught a tree branch hanging over the pond, putting a small gash in her knee. She pulled herself up by the branch and ran into the back door of the kitchen, trying to put up a brave front.

Cook was busy preparing lunch, but stopped when she saw the child's tear-stained face. Then she spotted the cut on her leg. Sitting her down on a chair, she wiped her face and leg with a wet cloth, got some liniment and a bandage from a kitchen cabinet and gently wrapped her leg.

Cook had always felt sorry for the child, and knew Mrs. Spencer would be furious with her daughter for disobeying.

The girl's mother came into the kitchen to check on her late lunch, and found Cook comforting her daughter. Dismissing her servant with a mere look, she took her daughter by the hand and led her into the parlor. The little girl trembled with fear, but her mother gathered her daughter up into her arms. She sat on the sofa and laid the child next to her, the girl's head resting on her mother's lap.

The mother softly kissed her daughter's cheek and stroked her hair. The little girl would never forget this moment. It was one of the few times her mother had ever shown her any affection. She'd soon fallen asleep at her mother's side.

Chapter 22

OVER A WEEK HAD PASSED since Violet had met with Frank at the Regis—eight days since she'd "botched" the stake-out. After her first cup of coffee, Violet decided to relax and read the Monday morning Times. She didn't have much use for the paper, and, admittedly, hadn't read the front page news since the war ended. She quickly turned to the society page and read the headlines. A picture of prominent Madison Avenue socialite, Sylvia Harrington, chairing New York City's Fifth Annual Firemen's Ball, caught her eye.

Violet pulled the newspaper closer to her face. Her coffee cup crashed to the floor. Sylvia Harrington was elegance, style and class—all rolled up into one—and Violet was positive she was the same gorgeous blonde she'd seen at the St. Regis hotel bar cozying up to that good looking sucker. She took a long, hard look at her face. Yep, she was the one. She'd know that face anywhere. She'd bet on it. Oh God, she had to talk to Frank. Would he believe her? Would Smallwood even listen to her after all the mistakes she'd made?

Violet's pulse quickened as she picked up the phone. An operator connected her to the station.

* * *

Frank and Bobby John sat together at his desk reviewing the timeline they'd set up for the hotel homicides. The telephone rang. Frank lifted the receiver.

"Frankie, it's Violet. I know you're mad, but don't hang up. I know who did it."

"Who did what?" Frank asked.

"You know—the dame that whacked those three chumps—you remember? The one I let get away!"

"How in the...what? Just where did you get that piece of information?"

"She's the headliner on today's society page, baby. None other than Mrs. Sylvia Harrington, wife of banker big shot, William Harrington."

Frank grabbed the newspaper spread out on his desk and fumbled for the society page. A voluptuous blonde stared back at him. "You gotta be kidding, Vi. You do know what you're saying, for Chrissakes?"

"Yep, I sure do, and I'm coming in to talk to you guys. Whadaya say... Duffy's in about an hour? You might want to talk to your boss first—you know—prepare him."

The phone went dead.

Frank tossed the newspaper to Bobby John and stabbed his finger at the radiant picture of Sylvia Harrington smiling for the cameras.

"You're not buying this, are you?" asked an incredulous Bobby John.

"Maybe Mrs. Harrington doesn't have it all."

"Man, are you kidding? She's rich and beautiful. She's got it made. What more does she want?"

"Maybe her husband beats her. Maybe he cheats on her. Maybe she's just plain crazy. Or maybe her glamorous life isn't what it's cracked up to be."

"So...Mr. Harrington just might be on her hit list. Is that what you're saying?"

"Now, who's the genius?"

"There's only one small problem," offered Bobby John.

"And what would that be?"

"Smallwood."

Frank sank into his chair, dumbfounded. How could this be? It was possible, but highly improbable. If it was true, he was pretty damn sure he knew who might be one of her victims. And this just couldn't happen, not if he had anything to say about it.

* * *

On a raw November morning, Violet put on her pale blue pleated skirt, donned her pillbox hat with wrap, hailed a cab, and headed for Duffy's. She was counting on her little bit of information being worth a pretty penny. She'd been stiffed by the cops with the St. Regis bust, but things were beginning to turn around for Frank's favorite snitch.

She smiled at Sylvia Harrington's picture, stuffed the New York Times into her purse, then walked into the bar. She had a story to tell...an unbelievable story. And Smallwood would listen. With no leads, little evidence and a serial killer loose on the city streets, he didn't have a choice.

Chapter 23

AFTER THE MEETING WITH VIOLET, Bobby John and Melvin split a platter of ribs and a couple of beers at a rib joint in Harlem. B.J. needed someone to talk to, and Melvin had become his confidante and trusted friend. Now, word on the street had it they needed to talk.

Melvin came out of the hotel after taking baggage to the front desk, and saw his friend sitting on the steps. He took a newspaper out of his inside jacket pocket—a paper he'd picked up at a newsstand on his way to work-- and sat next to Bobby.

"Looks like your little lady is making news again!" Melvin laughed, and handed Bobby John a wrinkled newspaper with a photograph of Sylvia Harrington. Splashed on the front page, she was being touted as a celebrity tennis player, winning money for charity. The close-up picture of the Madison Avenue socialite revealed her incredible beauty, as well as her upper body strength. The picture showed her slamming the ball out of the court, an impressive finish to the match. Sadly, her opponent had not scored a single point.

Bobby John realized Sylvia Harrington would have little trouble killing any man with her bare hands—let alone one she'd drugged. She wasn't just another pretty face with a gorgeous body; she was a merciless killer playing everyone for a fool. Now, Smallwood had to convince Delgado and everybody else that her husband might just be next, and they were running out of time. The clock was ticking and it had been over two weeks since the last hotel hit.

Bobby John and Frank agreed that her big-shot husband was actually helping Sylvia get away with murder because of his prominent position. But they also agreed that William Harrington probably wasn't the kind of guy who would finger his wife anyway. The negative publicity would've killed him before she even got to him.

Bobby John stared at the picture of the woman who had brought the entire N.Y.P.D. to its knees.

"Just look at the biceps on that dame."

Melvin nodded. "Yep, she could snap a neck real good with those muscles."

Bobby John didn't need convincing. He knew his friend was right.

Chapter 24

SMALLWOOD FOUND HIMSELF PACING back and forth in front of Commissioner Thomas Delgado's office. He'd arrived twenty minutes early, and with three homicides, one unbelievable lead and little evidence, he knew his boss would show no mercy.

The hallway was hot. Wiping beads of sweat from his forehead with his handkerchief—his damp shirt sticking to his back-- Smallwood loosened his tie and sat in one of the ancient wooden chairs across from the office. The imposing door, with its pebbled glass window, had once proudly displayed the commissioner's name in bold black letters, but unfortunately, his name, not to mention his reputation, was starting to fade.

Smallwood heard a heated discussion coming from Delgado's office, when a tearful secretary opened the door and quickly walked down the hallway, clutching a handkerchief.

"Next!" boomed a loud voice from the commissioner's office. Smallwood crossed the hall and entered the room with dread.

"Shit, it looks like I'll need another secretary. Nobody has a sense of humor anymore, if you know what I mean. Why don't ya sit down, Ron, and we'll see if you can make my day any more intolerable. I hope, for all of our sakes, there's not a fourth murder you're about to hit me with?"

A short, overweight man, Commissioner Delgado had red spider veins on a round, blotchy face. He was quick to anger, had a dry sense of humor, few friends and lots of enemies. According to office gossip, his ex-wife claimed he had a serious drinking problem.

Smallwood tentatively sat in the chair facing Delgado's desk. He didn't remember a time when the commissioner didn't have a cigar in his mouth, not smoking it, but chewing vigorously on the butt, as if it were something to be devoured.

Smallwood looked at his boss's large, wooden desk, askew with papers, a half-eaten plate of spaghetti and a multitude of tattered files. As usual, a large stogie was clenched between his coffee-stained teeth.

"This case is starting to look like a goddamn circus, Ron. Are you sure Kowalski's up to this? Maybe he's been nursing a bad leg for too damned long. And that negro fellow, Taylor; he's got a hot temper and doesn't like playing by the rules—or so I've heard. Just maybe we need some new guys on the case. Whadaya think, Ron? Because I'm running out of time and patience. One more thing. I understand there's a hooker somehow involved. Please tell me that isn't true. And also tell me why this little tidbit of information remains a secret to me and everyone else who has been crawling up my ass since the first murder?"

"You gotta hear me out, Tom."

"I already don't like the sound of it."

"It's Sylvia Harrington."

"*The* Sylvia Harrington! If this is a joke, look at me! I'm not laughing."

"Violet Zussman is ready to swear to it. She's positive she saw her at the Regis the night of the third murder. She corroborated it with a picture of Sylvia Harrington she cut out of The Time's society page."

"You mean that hooker who helped us with the Smithson case?"

"One and the same. Another thing; and you're not going to like this part, we think Sylvia Harrington's husband might be next."

"And just who's 'we?' Kowalski and that colored fella, Taylor?"

"Not exactly. Kowalski, Taylor, and yes—me."

Commissioner Delgado yanked the cigar from his mouth and stomped it into the worn, tile floor. "Well, well, if this ain't rich! You're telling me I'm going to call Mr. William Harrington, one of the biggest banking big shots in the city, and tell him his wife is a murderer? Oh, and by the way, sir, you just might be next! Is that what you're saying, Ron?"

"That's exactly what I'm saying, Tom."

"I've heard you out. Now, let me let you in on a little secret, Ron. If William Harrington is found with a noose around his neck anytime soon, you and your buddies can keep your jobs. But I must say, my friend, the odds aren't in your favor."

"Call me an optimist, Tom. But the way I see it, I think the odds look pretty damn good."

Chapter 25

SYLVIA STARED AT HER REFLECTION in her bedroom mirror. The clock on her bed-side table showed almost seven o'clock; time for her husband to come home for a late-night dinner. But she had other plans for the evening.

He'd been spending more and more time at the office, showing little or no interest in her, and she'd become increasingly resentful. She went into her closet and pulled out her most alluring dress.

She chose a black silk, ankle-length, with a revealing neckline. A slit up the side exposed her long, willowy legs. She slipped into the dress, touched up her make-up, and brushed her soft, blonde hair, allowing it to cascade down her back. On her way down the winding staircase to the front door, she heard her husband entering the house. She found him unbuttoning his coat in the entrance way.

He greeted her with a forced smile.

"You look stunning, my darling. What's the occasion?"

"We've spent so little time together lately. I thought I'd surprise you. I've made dinner reservations at The Mansfield, and reserved a luxurious suite for the night. No need to change; I've already arranged for a taxi to pick us up at seven thirty."

"I guess you won't take no for an answer. It has been a long week."

Sylvia pressed her body against him, touching his lips with her fingertips. "Shh, my darling. Just let me take care of you."

She buttoned up his topcoat, put on her favorite black sable and feathered tricorne hat and led him to the cab.

* * *

Mr. Harrington had one too many martinis at dinner, but Sylvia made sure to keep her wits about her by emptying her drinks into her water glass. When she saw her husband's eyes start to glaze, she put her plan into motion.

"Ty, sweetheart, I think it's time to call it a night. Here, let me help you."

He tried to stand, but staggered and nearly fell. Sylvia frowned, worried he was too intoxicated to walk to the elevator—even with her help—but she managed to get him into their room.

He would undoubtedly refuse another drink, so she laced a glass of water with the chloral hydrate. He sipped the cool water, while she lifted his feet onto the bed and fluffed the pillow behind his head.

"Is that better, dear?" she cooed into his ear.

"Yes, but could you at least let me take my shoes off?"

"Why don't you just leave everything to me?"

"I'm so tired...can't seem to..."

Sylvia sat beside her unsuspecting husband. "Here, loosen your tie. Let me help." She loosened his tie, but didn't remove it.

Ty tried to sit up in bed, clutching at her arm with a trembling hand. She looked at him with all the hatred she felt for his kind. His eyes widened in fear.

"If I tell you a secret, will you promise not to tell?" Sylvia whispered.

He nodded in agreement. "Of course, I would never tell, my darling."

Mr. Lindquist didn't kill my father. I did."

"You...I don't understand. That's not possible."

"Father was an evil man who did unspeakable things. His sordid relationships with other women were legend. And you, my beloved, have violated my trust for the last time, and sadly, must pay for your own infidelities."

Ty's eyes grew even wider. "You're the one. It was you. The newspaper accounts...the innocent men."

"Innocent? I think not."

"Sylvia straddled her husband, and, with gloved hands, tightened the tie around his neck with a strength that always surprised her. Minutes later, looking into his lifeless face, she checked for a pulse, found none, then closed his eyes with her fingertips.

As usual, she tidied up the room and wiped off the glasses, emptying the solitary ashtray on the bedside table. Sylvia felt uncharacteristically nervous, as she made her way to the bathroom. When she emptied the perfume bottle containing the deadly poison into the sink, it slipped from her hands and fell to the marble floor.

Thank God it didn't break, she whispered to herself. She scooped it up, hurriedly put the bottle back into her purse and left the hotel room.

Sylvia called for room service from the lobby's payphone, then strode outside to hail a cab. Confident that nothing had been left undone, she entered the waiting taxi and headed for home.

Stranglehold

Sylvia knew the hotel staff would soon find her husband's lifeless body. It shouldn't have ever happened. But her deceitful husband left her no choice. She undressed and slipped into bed. Trying to sleep, and fighting the demons, visions of her father ran through her mind. He also had left her no choice. What a pity.

* * *

At age fifteen, Sylvia was sick to death of the endless dinner parties in her home. She stood silently in the library doorway, listening to a heated argument between her father and his business partner, Mr. Lindquist. Her father beckoned her into the room, as Mr. Lindquist thumped his wine glass on a table, and stormed out of the room. He nodded at Sylvia as he slammed the door behind him.

Her father turned his back to her and tipped the ashes of his pipe into the roaring fireplace. She heard nothing of his mindless banter, and when he turned around, she stepped towards him, picked up an iron poker, and swung it at her father's head. It struck his neck with a dull thud. He screamed in pain and reeled forward, struggling to keep his balance. Her second blow crushed his skull. He dropped to his knees and fell face down on the floor, his blood staining the richly carpeted rug. Sylvia calmly removed the sash from her dress, wiped off her weapon, and stuffed the bloodied sash into her pocket.

When questioned by police, asking her if she knew of anyone who would commit such a heinous crime, Sylvia concealed a smile. Yes, of course, she knew who did it. Everyone heard them fighting at the dinner party earlier. It was Mr. Lindquist, her father's trusted business partner.

Chapter 26

VIOLET'S SUSPICIONS ABOUT SYLVIA HARRINGTON continued to haunt Frank. Her husband wasn't safe. But nobody was listening, except for Bobby John and Smallwood-- who was in deep shit with Commissioner Delgado.

Frank fell asleep on the sofa around ten o'clock, clutching yet another newspaper account of socialite Sylvia Harrington's raising money for the city's poor and downtrodden. Her shameless husband stood beside her like a faithful dog. Frank studied William, "Ty" Harrington's well-chiseled features—prominent jaw, cleft chin, and dazzling smile—before he closed his eyes for a well-deserved sleep. He awoke to someone banging on his front door.

"I'm comin' already; don't break it down, for Chrissakes," Frank yelled as he struggled to the front door. He hit the porch light, revealing Bobby John standing in the doorway.

"I don't even want to know how you got here."

"I hate to bother you like this, Frankie, but I got something that won't wait. I couldn't sleep, and if I know you, I bet you're not sleeping too good either."

"Don't worry about it. You're right. Haven't slept worth a damn in weeks. Come on in. Please don't tell me we have another body?"

"You know that friend of mine, Melvin, the doorman at The Mansfield? Last week he showed me a picture of Mrs. Harrington. I stopped by the hotel tonight to see if he'd seen anything and he swore he saw her and a man at the hotel tonight—saw 'em checking in and everything. The best part is he saw her get into a cab—alone—around midnight. Worth checking into, right?"

"Yeah, but something tells me Mrs. Harrington's gotten away with murder...again."

* * *

Around one-thirty, Frank and Bobby John entered a lobby crawling with cops and several reporters who'd got wind of yet another hotel murder. The man at the front desk looked up at the detectives with a sour expression.

"I believe you're looking for room six ten, gentlemen; the Harrington suite. But I'm afraid you're much too late to be of any help."

Frank and B.J. got in the elevator and took it to the sixth floor without speaking a word. Frank opened the door, and saw the crew already working the case—Sam Giordano, Smallwood, and several lab technicians waiting to get in on the action.

Frank slowly approached the bed, his eyes riveted to the body in front of him. William Harrington was lying down, fully dressed, shoes on, with the familiar noose around a bloated neck. It was all he could do not to grab the body by the throat and scream, "You stupid sonofabitch! Didn't you see it coming?" But he knew better than to touch the body, and this corpse, regretfully, had nothing to say.

Captain Smallwood walked up to Frank and placed his hand on his shoulder. "I should've believed you and

Bobby John. You were right. And Violet was right, for God's sake. But the one and only Sylvia Harrington is going to get away with this. She's going to claim that her louse of a husband bedded a serial killer and got what was coming to him."

Frank said nothing, but knew Smallwood was right.

* * *

"Shit, this room is wiped clean...nothin'. Don't think she's been gone long," Bobby John muttered. The bathroom light, still on, gave him an uneasy feeling. He wandered into the room and a small shard of sparkling glass on the floor caught his eye.

"Boss, I think I got something." Bobby John crouched down on the bathroom floor, and, with a gloved hand, picked up a miniature glass swan, tiny pieces of blue glass still attached. "Looks like it broke off the top of something."

Frank and the captain walked in. "And it looks like evidence," Frank said. .

Captain Smallwood knelt beside Bobby John. "Good job, son, and I mean it."

"Don't give me credit too soon."

Smallwood stood and put his hand on Frank's shoulder.

"I'm afraid Mr. Harrington's death is no coincidence. I'm going to get a search warrant for the Harrington mansion to look for the evidence we need to crack this case. We're going to play everything by the book, boys, and we're going to catch ourselves a killer. But first I'm going to pay a visit to Tom Delgado's office and wipe that smug look off his face. Because it looks like we're still in business."

Chapter 27

FRANK AND BOBBY JOHN PULLED UP in front of the Harrington brownstone around noon— just days before Christmas. Frank was nervous as hell, but tried not to show it. He carried the search warrant that would hopefully give them the clue they needed to break the case.

"Bobby, let me ask the questions. You get into her bedroom and grab some shoes—lots of shoes. And you have to find her purse."

"I got it covered, Boss, but maybe she won't talk. Have you thought of that?"

"Oh, she'll talk. I'm sure she doesn't wanna take the ride down to the station where things wouldn't be so pretty. She'll feel safe controlling the situation right in her own home."

The Harrington house was one of the most striking homes in Gramercy Park—known for its lavish parties and celebrity guests. Frank and Bobby John walked up the steps leading to the stately residence and rang the doorbell. After a lengthy wait, a disgruntled maid answered the door.

Frank flashed the warrant. "Ma'am, Detective Kowalski and my partner, Detective Taylor. We're here to see Mrs. Harrington about her husband's recent death."

The maid frowned. "Follow me, please."

She escorted them to a large sitting room, filled with luxurious rugs, priceless paintings and antique furniture. Even in the dead of winter, fresh flowers sat on every table in the room.

"It don't look much like the home of a serial killer," offered a somber Bobby John.

"Yeah, let's make this short and sweet; we don't want to make this woman think we're interested in anything but getting some facts straight. I'll start with the simple questions and then hit her with the hard ones. As far as she knows, searching the premises is just part of our job."

* * *

A few minutes later, Sylvia Harrington made her way down the winding staircase. Frank and Bobby John were immediately struck by her beauty. The newspapers didn't do her justice. She was simply stunning.

Bobby John knew better than to stare. A colored man could easily get himself lynched for that mistake.

Sylvia's long platinum blonde hair sat at the nape of her neck, loosely tied in a knotted chignon. Her chartreuse dressing gown revealed a more than ample bosom and slender legs visible from a long slit on the side. She approached them as if to consume them with a single look.

The maid offered a simple introduction, then dismissed herself.

"Gentlemen, how may I help you? I'm afraid you've picked quite a busy day for me, so if we may get started? I'm meeting with my late husband's lawyer later this afternoon to review his will and estate."

Sylvia Harrington appeared calm and composed. She stared disapprovingly at Bobby John.

Frank cleared his throat. "We're here with a search warrant, ma'am."

"I see...a search warrant." Her eyes twinkled with amusement. "Search away, gentlemen. However, I do have a problem with this colored man touching my things."

Bobby John's anger welled up inside of him, but he kept it in check. No way in hell would he mess up this investigation.

"This colored man is my partner, Detective Bobby John Taylor, and I assure you he will handle your things with the utmost respect. We'll need to see your bedroom."

Sylvia Harrington called her maid back, and B. J. offered a weak smile as she led him up the stairway and through the French doors leading to the master bedroom suite.

* * *

Meanwhile, Sylvia offered Frank a chair directly across from her in the living room.

Frank sat, and several uncomfortable minutes passed before he began.

"Nice place."

"Thank you."

"I need to ask you a few questions regarding your husband's death. Routine police procedures, ma'am."

"Of course."

"Where were you on the night of your husband's murder?"

"I was at home. My husband hadn't come home from work; it was late, so I dined alone. I assumed he was meeting with clients, or having a late night dinner with a business partner. I went to bed around ten."

"Is there anyone to corroborate your testimony?"

"Unfortunately, no. I sent my staff home early."

"Did your husband have any enemies that you know of?"

"Not that I'm aware of. I'm sure you have enemies, Detective."

"If you mean enemies that want to see me dead—not many."

Frank took a deep breath.

"To your knowledge, has your husband ever cheated on you?"

"That's absolutely ridiculous."

"Was your husband having any problems with any business associates or partners?"

"Not that I'm aware of."

"Did you and your husband have any problems in your marriage?"

"All married couples have an occasional spat, Detective, but I assure you we had no marital difficulties."

"I know this is difficult, Mrs. Harrington, but did you kill your husband?"

"That's absurd! Why would I kill him?"

"My guess is because he has cheated on you— probably more than once—and it's time to get even."

Sylvia stood abruptly.

"I resent this line of questioning. I'm afraid I have nothing more to say, Detective Kowalski. I only hope you find out who did kill my husband, and make them pay for this unspeakable crime."

"Right. I guess I'm finished for now, ma'am. Would you mind waiting just a few more minutes for my partner? I'm sure he'll be down soon."

"Fine…a few minutes."

"I'm sorry if I offended you, Mrs. Harrington, but rest assured, nobody gets away with murder on my watch…nobody."

Sylvia Harrington's answers had been cold and emotionless; her statements calculated and of little help to Frank. He hoped Bobby John was having better luck upstairs.

* * *

Bobby knew he didn't have a lot of time and he had to play by the rules. He was putting on gloves, when he spotted a black sable coat draped over a lounge chair next to the bed. He methodically removed several strands, placed them in an evidence bag from his jacket pocket and labeled it. Mrs. Harrington's unopened purse lay on the bed. He opened it and found it empty. Bobby John's heart sank. There was more work to do.

He made his way to Sylvia's walk-in closet. Bobby John hadn't seen so many shoes in his entire life. He couldn't take them all. The shoes in the back of the closet, meticulously arranged on a long metal rack and covered in plastic, clearly hadn't been worn for awhile. He took eight left shoes from the ones that looked most used—hoping that one of them would match the partial left shoeprint lifted from the St. Regis—and put them in a pillowcase taken from her bed.

He was about to leave, disappointed at not finding the purse that could connect her to the murders, when Bobby John noticed the portrait of Sylvia Harrington hanging over the bed— a younger version of the woman he'd just met for the first time. Her face had a beautiful, yet sad expression. And in spite of it all, he felt a twinge of sympathy for this heartless woman.

The picture sat slightly crooked on the wall. Remembering seeing a movie once where some mobster stashed his money behind a picture over a mantle, he reached behind the picture. His fingers brushed a large knob.

Heart pounding, he removed the portrait and found a metal safe hidden behind it— locked, of course. Bobby John had some experience cracking safes in his younger days, but time was against him. He had to work fast. With hands trembling, he held his ear to the tumbler, and carefully turned it back and forth, listening to the almost inaudible "clicks" until he finally opened the safe.

Inside, he found several documents, large amounts of cash, several pieces of loose jewelry and a black purse. He dumped the contents of the purse on the bed: a hairbrush, a jeweled lipstick case, a St. Regis matchbook and a bloodied handkerchief concealing a broken perfume bottle. Bobby John figured she must have cut herself reaching inside the purse. It was all beginning to make sense. He carefully put the bottle back into the handkerchief and placed it in his inside jacket pocket. Satisfied he was done after bagging and labeling the purse's contents, he put the empty purse back into the safe and left the room as he found it.

When Bobby John descended the staircase, Sylvia glared at him and eyed her pillowcase with curiosity.

"Did you find anything at all that was helpful in your 'search', Detective Taylor?" Sylvia asked with a cynical smile.

"Yes, ma'am; you've been very helpful and I do thank you." B.J. tried to hide his excitement and it obviously worked. Frank looked both tired and defeated after grilling the stone-cold Mrs. Harrington.

"We'll be in touch, ma'am. Please don't leave the country, or plan any trips for the time being," Frank said, as they headed for the front door.

"Oh, I guess you haven't read the papers. I'm having a dinner party next week at my Hampton home on Christmas Eve. I plan to personally thank all of those who have been so supportive since my husband's death. I really don't plan on going anywhere, Detective Kowalski."

"We had to take some of your shoes, ma'am…and a pillowcase," Bobby John blurted out.

Sylvia smiled. "Don't worry, Detective, you've taken nothing that can't be replaced."

* * *

"What a damned waste of time! I got nothing…nothing from that lying bitch," Frank grumbled, as they walked to the cruiser.

"You didn't expect a confession, did ya?"

"Nah, I just wanted to trip her up—catch her in a lie, but she outsmarted me."

"The one and only Frank Kowalski?"

"Yeah, who woulda thought." They pulled away.

"So—whadaya think?" Frank added.

"I think that Harrington dame has a helluva lot of shoes."

"No, besides that. Maybe you got something there besides shoes."

"You trust me, right?"

"Of course I trust you. Do you even have to ask?"

"Because I mighta' found something that just might bust this case wide open."

"And that would be what?"

Silence.

"Are you kidding? You're really going to keep it from me? You do know it's illegal to withhold evidence—especially from your partner."

"You gonna turn me in? I think you can wait 'til tomorrow morning when we meet with Sam and Smallwood to go over the evidence. Look, I got the shoes, lots of shoes. I got hair from a fur coat, a lipstick case, a St. Regis matchbook with missing matches, and somethin' from a purse that oughta do the trick. You just gotta trust me on this one. Everything's in the back seat, all bagged and labeled. Drop it off for Sammy. It ought to keep 'em busy for awhile. And try to get some sleep tonight, Frankie. Looks like you need it."

"And just how am I supposed to sleep?"

"Everything's in the back seat."

"Almost everything," Frank sighed.

"And you trust me, right?"

"And I trust you."

* * *

Bobby tried to make small talk on the way back home, but Frank wasn't in the mood for conversation. He was angry he couldn't get any information from the shrewd Madison Avenue socialite. And if that wasn't enough, Bobby John's cat and mouse game with a crucial piece of evidence thoroughly pissed him off.

He reached Bobby John's neighborhood around five.

Bobby John jumped out of the cruiser and slammed the door, looking back at Frank's dejected face. He stuck his head into the window.

"You're not gonna let this go, are ya?"

"I just need to know, that's all."

"Then I'll tell ya'."

Bobby John recounted finding the bloodied handkerchief containing the broken perfume bottle.

"Are ya happy now?"

"Yeah…I'm happy as hell."

Bobby John smiled at his partner and headed for home.

"Pick me up by eight."

Chapter 28

BOBBY JOHN AWOKE WITH A START. Sweating and gasping for air, he kicked off the covers, remembering the dream that woke him up. Sylvia Harrington was standing over his bed in a white, flowing gown—arms outstretched—beckoning him to follow her.

Happy to be awake, B.J. reached over to the chair next to his bed and felt the inside pocket of his jacket. Yeah, the broken perfume bottle was still safe in his possession— the final piece of evidence that was sure to put Mrs. Harrington away for the rest of her life. He wasn't afraid to admit that he wanted his moment of glory.

Bobby John hoped that between the press and the department, Frank wouldn't get all the credit for bringing Sylvia Harrington down, but life had taught him not to expect too much from a white man's world. He sank down into his bed. It was too early to get up, but he was too wound-up to sleep. He pulled the covers over his head, waiting for the sun to come up.

* * *

He and Frank were meeting with Giordano and Smallwood first thing to discuss all the evidence gotten so far—most importantly— the items retrieved from the search of the Harrington home. Last week Giordano had been quick to point out that things didn't look too good.

Smallwood was more than impatient and running out of bullshit stories for Commissioner Delgado. Hopefully, things were about to change.

Frank and Bobby John entered Giordano's lab shortly after nine. Smallwood was waiting for them. He let it be known he wasn't interested in small talk.

"Well, if it ain't Abbott and Costello," Sam bellowed, as Frank and B.J. approached two large tables holding one pillowcase stuffed with shoes, and six opened evidence bags. Frank's eyes were glued to the small glass bird Bobby John lifted from the Mansfield.

"Yeah, you two make quite a pair," Smallwood said sarcastically.

Giordano spoke first. "Let's get busy, gentlemen, and let me be perfectly honest about the evidence we have so far. The black hair lifted from the hotels and the Harrington bedroom are consistent with those from almost any black sable coat worn by almost any rich broad in the city. The partial muddied shoeprint from the Regis is consistent with a left high-heeled shoe taken from the home, but it's not a match, due to the condition of the print. The small traces of blood found in her purse could have a reasonable explanation. Remember, this woman is smart.

We still can't figure out what the stupid glass bird has to do with any of this—if anything. The single match taken from the carpet of the Regis is the only thing we have to go on and that's shaky, even with the matchbook. It just doesn't look good, boys." Giordano shook his head.

"So, what you're saying is that this bitch, the one and only Sylvia Harrington, walks, because our evidence just isn't good enough?" asked an incredulous Smallwood.

"That's about it."

"Maybe this would help." B.J. pulled the broken perfume bottle out of his pocket. "I found this in Mrs. Harrington's purse yesterday—a purse inside a safe. It's got traces of chloral hydrate in it. Check it out."

"Bobby, this woman is clever. If this case went to court, she could have her doctor testify that chloral hydrate was prescribed for insomnia and that would be the end of it. Putting it in an empty perfume bottle and carrying it in her purse is no crime I know of," Sam said. "And it wouldn't put her at the scene of any murder—let alone her husband's murder."

Frank walked over to the table and picked up the glass bird, pieces of broken glass still attached to its bottom. All eyes watched, as Bobby John joined him. With a steady hand, Bobby took the miniature swan from his partner and placed it atop the neck of the bottle—the tiny glass shards fitting neatly into place. A perfect fit.

"The way I see it, this puts Sylvia Harrington in her husband's hotel room the night of the murder," offered a sober B.J.

Frank grinned. "And finally we can put her away for the rest of her stinking life."

"Am I in friggin' heaven, or what?" An elated Sam Giordano sank into his chair.

"I gotta tell you, Frank; you looked pretty surprised when Bobby John pulled that broken perfume bottle out of his pocket," said Smallwood.

"I'll tell you what, Captain. This guy never fails to amaze me, but it was no surprise."

"When we were searching the Harrington place, Frankie encouraged me to take the lead and I did. He

99

gets the hunch, I chase it down, and we get the job done."

Frank beamed. "And that, my friends, is what makes it work."

Smallwood put his arm around his two detectives and gave a solemn smile. "Well, boys, then I guess it's time for an arrest. Go get her, gentlemen."

Chapter 29

ON CHRISTMAS EVE, Frank and Bobby John drove in silence along the Long Island shoreline and headed for the Hamptons, leaving the city lights behind. Approximately two hours later, at eight P.M., they pulled up in front of the East Hampton address on Lily Pond Lane, the Harrington's second home.

Mrs. Harrington, the heartbroken widow, was throwing a lavish holiday party to assure friends and family she was "holding up," in spite of the family's recent tragedy. Frank parked his cruiser in front of the house, wedged between two limos. Many luxury cars, as well as several limousines, lined the exclusive neighborhood street. Bobby finally broke the ice.

"I guess playing the grieving widow just ain't her style," he said sarcastically.

Frank sighed. "Yeah, and it all comes down to this—taking her in at her own home." He already felt that familiar knot in the pit of his stomach and his leg hurt like hell. "I wonder if she'll give us any trouble."

"Nah, I think she knows we're coming for her. Look—she coulda split and she didn't."

Frank got out of the cruiser, clutching the arrest warrant that would close one of the most infamous serial murder cases in New York's history. Bobby John followed close behind.

"Before we crash the party, let's go around back and check the exits," he said.

"I thought you said she was waiting for us—no trouble, no problem."

"Yeah, but it wouldn't hurt to check just in case, right?"

A hesitant Frank agreed.

They found the yards at the back of the house protected by a large iron gate with a padlock. Bobby John quickly smashed the rusty lock with his service revolver. A nervous Frank shot him a worried glance.

"You wanna get in, or what?"

After passing through the gate, they stepped onto a patio with a stone walkway leading to a swimming pool about sixty feet from the house. A guest house sat to the right of the pool. Lush gardens enveloped the spacious yard, their leaves laden with new-fallen snow.

Frank and Bobby also noticed two sets of French doors on the ground level, all leading to the pool and gardens—potential getaways for Sylvia.

* * *

They walked to the front of the house and rang the doorbell. An obliging butler answered the door and escorted them into an extravagant party, even by Harrington standards. Close to fifty smartly dressed people, women dripping in pearls, milled around the large marble hallway, chattering and laughing— unaware of the two uninvited party crashers.

Champagne flowed from a large glass fountain, meticulously cut in the shape of a cherub. Polite maids in starched, white aprons, served caviar on silver platters. The succulent smell of smoked ham and turkey wafted from the kitchen—its tables laden with fruit pies, cakes and pastries.

A fire roared in the fireplace, its mantle adorned with holly berries and fragrant pinecones. A violin quartet assembled in the mezzanine above the hallway played holiday music.

Frank and Bobby John pushed their way through the throngs of people, and, as they wound their way through the crowd, spotted Sylvia Harrington. She was entertaining a few of her guests with what seemed to be an amusing story. Sylvia's long, blonde hair was swept up with a diamond-encrusted comb, revealing her creamy, white shoulders. She wore a simple red dress that fit her like a second skin.

Sylvia's guests excused themselves when they saw two men in brown suits and fedoras approaching their hostess with grim looks on their faces.

"Detective Kowalski, Detective Taylor, I was beginning to wonder what was taking you two boys so long," said a demure Sylvia.

Stunned, Frank flashed the warrant. "Ma'am, Sylvia Harrington, we're here to arrest you for the murders of one Michael Bollinger, one Rodney Davis and one Thomas Douglas, as well as the murder of your husband, William Harrington. I'm afraid you'll have to come with us."

She didn't even raise an eyebrow, just said, "Do you mind if I use the ladies' room first? I promise not to keep you waiting."

"Not at all, ma'am; just don't take too long," Bobby John said.

The flabbergasted guests watched in silence, as Sylvia crossed the room and entered the bathroom. Time slowly passed; Frank looked at his watch.

"Boss, she's taking just a little too long, if you ask me."

Frank nodded.

Bobby bolted for the bathroom, with Frank not far behind.

"Kick the door in!" Frank yelled.

Bobby John kicked in the door, only to find an open bathroom window, and a cruel wind howling through the room. The waste basket that had engineered Sylvia's escape, sat under the window.

"She's gone, Frankie!"

"By God, not if I can help it!"

The concerned party goers stared in morbid curiosity and blindly followed the officers, as they rushed to the front of the house. Frank and Bobby John ran out the door and headed for their cruiser, just as Sylvia's Buick Phaeton screamed down the driveway like a bright, yellow streak, headed for coastal highway twenty-seven.

Sylvia's guests spilled out over the lawn in their evening wear— a few men struggling into their top coats. Some women had grabbed their fur coats to ward off the bitter cold. A babble of loud voices pierced the usually quiet Hamptons neighborhood, people talking amongst themselves in disbelief. Quick to crucify Sylvia for her apparent crimes, the unforgiving guests walked back to the house to warm themselves, have another drink, and gossip about the scandalous story sure to make front page news.

* * *

"Get in, I'm driving," yelled Bobby John."

Frank ran close behind. "I'm not arguing!"

"Just trust me, Frankie."

"Like I have a choice."

Bobby John shot down the road and onto the deserted highway.

"Can you see her?" Frank shouted.

"Not yet; hold on!"

Bobby John trounced on the accelerator, pushing the cruiser to almost eighty miles per hour. A moment later, Frank caught sight of Sylvia's convertible going full throttle down the two-lane highway. The dark night gave way to a full moon, throwing light on her car and the road which had become a narrow ribbon.

"We need to scare her; shake her up a little!" Frank cried. "Get on her bumper and don't let up until she gets tired and slows down."

Three miles later, with frazzled nerves and a relentless woman behind the wheel of the get-away car, Frank decided on a new tactic.

"Frankie, she's not going to give it up!" Bobby John shrieked.

"Yeah, I get it! Keep up your speed and get on the driver's side of her car and hit it—hit it hard. Back off and do it again! She's either going to brake, crash, or pull off the road. Then, by God, we got her!"

The smell of burning rubber and motor oil seared their lungs. Sylvia slowed down to a mere seventy miles per hour, careening around a sharp curve. Bobby John pulled up beside the luxury convertible. Brakes squealing, he dropped to the same speed, then repeatedly rammed her car, allowing her no time to strike back.

Frank looked in her window at the unyielding woman behind the wheel. She gripped the steering wheel, eyes straightforward and apparently unshaken. Briefly, she turned to look at them, piercing them with her steel blue eyes. Frank thought he saw the devil himself in that glance, and he was scared to death. But Bobby John's focus jolted him back to reality.

After their cars collided for the fourth time, Sylvia's convertible skidded off the highway with what appeared to be a flat tire. This was the break they were looking for.

Frank and Bobby John jumped out of the cruiser, while Sylvia less than two hundred feet away, slowly opened the driver's side door and climbed out, appearing unruffled by the recent turn of events. Wearing only her red silk dress and high-heels, she calmly reached into the passenger's side and pulled out her husband's German Luger. She fired a shot at her would-be captors, only managing to hit the windshield of their already battered cruiser.

"Shit, Frankie, she's got a gun!"

"Yeah, but luckily for us, she's a bad shot."

Sylvia dropped the semi-automatic pistol on the ground, and poised as usual, stepped out of her shoes, and ran to the side of the road leading to the ocean. She climbed down the embankment that met with massive rocks. Angry waves pounded them with incredible force. A full moon captured the silhouette of a determined Sylvia trying to climb out to the rocks to safety.

Bobby John followed right behind her, as Frank anxiously watched from the road.

B.J. climbed out onto a large boulder and attempted to reason with her, screaming her name. The cold, winter wind all but drowned out his voice.

"Mrs. Harrington, please… stop! Let us help you. You don't need to do this. I can help. You must be cold. Here, take my jacket."

"I don't need your help," Sylvia cried out.

"You sure about that?" Bobby John shouted.

She turned to face him, lost her balance and stumbled on a slippery rock— her foot wedged between two large boulders.

"She's down, Frank!"

Bobby John lost his footing more than once, before he reached her sitting on a rock, blood running down her leg, with waves about to throw her into the frigid water. He took off his jacket and secured it around her shoulders, while trembling with cold. Sylvia stared blankly into his eyes. B. J. ripped a large piece of fabric from his shirt, wrapped it around her foot, and wiggled it back and forth until her injured foot came free.

Sylvia attempted to get up. She winced in pain, but showed no other emotion.

Bobby John reached down to grab her hand, but she recoiled in disgust.

"So, this is the way you want to play it?" Bobby John yelled in anger.

Once again, he reached down, but instead of taking her hand, he grabbed the comb holding her long hair in place. As it tumbled around her shoulders, he snatched a large lock of it and wrapped it around his hand.

"Look, I can drag you over the rocks by the hair, or you can take my hand and walk back up without a fight. It really don't matter to me."

Reluctantly, she took Bobby John's hand, and they slowly maneuvered their way up the rocks to safety.

Frank was waiting at the top of the embankment, scared to death, but happy to see his partner, with Sylvia Harrington in tow.

"You crazy son-of-a-bitch!"

"I deserve that, but I knew she didn't want to die, and I sure as hell didn't want to die saving her."

"Here, put my coat on. You're freezing to death," Frank said. "I'll get her in the car and I'll drive. A hospital needs to check you both out before we book her."

Bobby John looked at Sylvia in the rear view mirror and thought he saw tears in her eyes. Her eyes met his, and though wet and bedraggled, she quickly regained her composure.

"Have you no manners, Detective Taylor? I suppose you were never taught that it is quite impolite to stare."

"Damn woman! I think you sound pretty ungrateful to someone who just saved your miserable life!"

"I'm so very sorry, but you'll get no thanks from me."

"Suit yourself. Do you think we ought to cuff her, Frankie? You know...with her history and all."

"Why didn't I think of that?"

"Maybe because I'm finally smarter than you."

Chapter 30

It promised to be one helluva Christmas Eve. The grandkids were running around the house, his son-in-law was getting plastered, and Ron Smallwood was watching a clock on the mantle with hands that never seemed to move. He really needed a bourbon and water to settle his nerves; that should do the trick. It was past midnight. Frank should have called by now. Sweet mother of God; what if something went wrong—horribly wrong? Frank had certainly made his share of mistakes. And if Bobby John screwed it up, he'd never hear the end of it. Delgado already told him their heads would once again be on the chopping block if they didn't make an arrest.

What if she got away? But where would she go? A light snow was starting to fall.

Smallwood was in the middle of fixing himself a stiff drink, when the telephone rang. Ann frantically cleared the living room—herding everyone back into the kitchen for yet more food.

"Boss, we got her," Frank said, without any hint of emotion in his voice.

Smallwood slipped into his easy chair, breathing a long sigh of relief.

"You taking her downtown?"

"You really didn't think *the* Sylvia Harrington was going down without a fight, did you?"

"Yeah, I guess that was too much to ask for, but that doesn't answer my question."

"After I told her we were taking her in, she excused herself to go to the ladies' room, climbed out of a bathroom window, and got away in her sports car."

"And you caught her?"

"Only after Bobby John chased her for close to five miles at eighty miles an hour, ramming her car, until, thankfully, she got a flat tire and skidded off highway twenty-seven."

"Sweet Jesus. And then you got her, right?"

"Not exactly. She climbed out of the car, reached for a Luger on the seat and took her best shot. Just lucky for us she couldn't shoot straight."

"So you disarmed her and got her in the cruiser?"

"This is where it gets really interesting."

"Shit."

"Mrs. Harrington managed to climb down the embankment, headed for the water and stumbled on a rock. Bobby John was right behind her, trying to reason with her. But she wasn't about to listen. That's when he decided to give her a choice."

"And that would be...?"

"To take his hand and walk back together peacefully, or be dragged by the hair to dry land. Let's just say she knew it was over and took his advice."

"My God, is he all right?"

"Cold and a little shaken up, but fine. I'm taking him to the hospital to be on the safe side. Looks like Mrs. Harrington's going to be admitted, checked out and released to police custody."

"Frank—a damn good piece of police work. I mean it. As for Bobby John, I know I've been hard on him. But you and I know there was a lot at stake here."

"Ron, I knew he had it in him."

"And now I'm a believer."

"That was the plan."

* * *

Smallwood hung up the phone, walked over to the living room window and parted the curtains. It had stopped snowing and glistening white snow blanketed his lawn. Tonight had turned into quite a night.

Ann came out of the kitchen and walked up behind him, gently slipping her arms around her husband's waist.

"Is it over?"

"Yeah, it's over. They got her. But not without a fight."

He recounted the story ending with the option to take B.J.'s hand or be dragged by the hair.

"I take it she gave up after being given that choice?"

"Against her will, but yeah. And I wasn't going to tell you this, but that crazy bitch even tried to shoot them after she went off the road!"

"Oh my God! But they're okay, right?"

"They're both fine; trust me."

"Don't you have something to say to me, Ronnie?"

"Frank is one helluva cop."

"And…"

"And—Bobby John is a damned hero—and yeah, you told me so."

Ann softly kissed his neck and tightened her arms around her husband's waist.

Epilogue

IT WAS AN EARLY SPRING DAY and a chilly rain was starting to fall. A blanket of umbrellas filled the churchyard as people began pouring into Ebenezer Baptist Church to honor one of their own. Bobby John Taylor hadn't set foot in this church since he'd been "washed in the blood of Jesus" as a young boy, but that made little or no difference to those who congregated there.

The choir was getting warmed up, and Bobby John attempted to straighten his tie for the hundredth time. His chest filled with pride; he looked in the front pew and saw Beverly in her navy blue tweed suit. His two young boys squirmed in their seats, dressed in their Sunday best. Even Uncle Louis showed up, and that meant a lot.

Bobby's eyes nervously scanned the congregation, looking for his friend. It wasn't hard to spot Frank. His was the only white face among hundreds of others.

Bobby John had been given a decent raise and the promise of a promotion by Smallwood, a man he'd come to trust and respect. He'd even moved out of the "rat hole." Things were looking up for his family and Beverly was finally talking to him.

* * *

Frank felt more than a little uncomfortable, realizing he hadn't been in a church since he lost his wife almost two

112

years ago. He felt all eyes on him, as he found a pew toward the middle of the church. Some looked in curiosity, some in anger, and even a few with guarded smiles. But they all looked. Frank realized he must be the first white man to ever set foot there, but hopefully not the last. Frank was the chosen one, hand-picked by the captain of Harlem's Thirty-Fourth, to award Bobby John the Medal of Valor.

Frank had received almost all the credit for solving one of the most notorious crime sprees in the city's history. The newspapers barely mentioned Bobby John's name and his courageous rescue of the undeserving killer. But word of Bobby John's selfless act spread quickly through the streets of Harlem.

Frank had been given a big raise, and promoted to Detective First Class. He'd vowed to keep Bobby John with him at the Twentieth, and he was, if nothing else, a man of his word. Amid the cries of "amen" and the glorious gospel music, Frank heard a booming voice call out his name. He took a deep breath and made his way to the front of the church. This time he didn't have a pounding headache; his stomach wasn't in knots and his leg didn't hurt. Frank was ready.

As he headed down the aisle, people turned their heads towards the back of the church. The steel hinges on the two massive wooden doors clanked loudly. Something or someone was trying to get in. The silence was deafening as the anxious congregation held their breaths, frozen with fear.

Unexpectedly, the heavy doors creaked open, flanked by two police officers of the Twentieth. In a somber expression of solidarity, the rest of the officers, led by Ron Smallwood and Johnny Zimmerman, quietly took their seats at the back of the church. It was a

glorious sight, church pews spilling over with men who
had come to pay tribute to their hero.

THE END

Acknowledgments

Stranglehold led me on an incredible journey. Through all of its twists, turns and endless revisions, I stayed faithful to its original plot and characters. But I couldn't have completed it without the many people who traveled with me along the way.

I wish to thank Round Hill Writer's Group, Round Hill, Virginia, whose members have always been there to support and encourage me. Bobbi Carducci, founder of this gifted group of local writers, has been a steadfast friend, in addition to providing me insight as an accomplished writer and author.

I would also like to thank Pennwriter's, Inc., whose writing conferences, with its many talented members and contributors, made me a better writer.

David Eno, retired Assistant Commissioner of Prisons for the state of New York, as well as the former president of the Federal Criminal Investigator's Association in Washington, D.C., was my beta reader, pointing out the inconsistencies in my writing. He offered the proper terminology used by urban police departments in the 1940's, and his fascinating anecdotes regarding police life in that era also provided invaluable back-story to my novella.

My uncle, David P. Grimes, retired F.B.I. Agent, assisted me in documenting correct police protocol and procedures used in post-war America. This book is lovingly dedicated to him, who, sadly, died before it was published.

I also wish to extend my gratitude to my friend, Chris James, who never stopped believing in me.

I am grateful to my husband, Mark, and my children, Ben and Libbey, who encouraged me to complete it, when I often found myself disheartened and about to give up.

I am also indebted to my friend and publisher, Dixiane Hallaj, who liked my story and took a chance with me.

Many thanks go to Tahlia Newland, the remarkable woman who edited my book. And special thanks to Kevin Berry, my proofreader.

Finally, I would like to express my humble appreciation to Frank Kowalski, *Stranglehold's* super sleuth, whose continuous voice in my head, along with his signature grit, determination and sense of humor, pushed me to completion of this novella.

About the Author

Ms. Grimes writes children's books and historical mysteries, as well as human interest short stories. She lives on a small horse farm in western Loudoun County, Virginia with her husband, Mark. She has two grown children.

Did you enjoy *Stranglehold*?

Please leave a review.

www.ingramcontent.com/pod-product-compliance
Lightning Source LLC
Chambersburg PA
CBHW050738230626
47052CB00003BA/516